Len McCawley

Bardo Boy

Len McCawley

Published in the USA
Copyright © Len McCawley 2009

This is a work of fiction.
All names, character, places and incidents, other than those
which are public domain, are the product of the author's imagi-
nation or are used fictitiously and any resemblance to actual persons, living or dead, businesses, events, or locales is entirely co-
incidental.

First published in the United States September 2009
ISBN 1449502636
EAN-13 9781449502638

Len McCawley grew up being entertained by stories about deceased relatives, how they died and the miracles surrounding their deaths. "It wasn't a holiday without a trip to the cemetery..." A family photo will often show a smiling baby planted in front of a tombstone.

Len's own paranormal experiences opened his mind to the many levels of reality that exist. Bardo Boy is glimpse into one of those worlds. He is currently working on Heruka, the second book in the Bardo Boy series.

Dear Bill,

Thanks for letting me use your photograph for the Book! Does the locker scene sound familiar?

Love
Limy

Two souls lost in the afterlife, one has the power to reunite them. Bardo Boy starts out as dead poet with amnesia. He is then resurrected in the afterlife as a Blood Drinker, with his memory restored and new abilities he begins his poetic search for his deceased lover, Drew.

Bardo Boy's quest for Drew takes him on a hallucinogenic journey through emotional and sexual adventures. This, Buddha meets Vampire, tale exists on multiple levels of reality. More than anything, it's a story about a love shared by two men that outshines life and death.

"...Remember the Universe's unfolding is perfection incarnate, it is our view of the unfolding that is flawed."- The Book of Bardo

For Jakob, Jason, and Karlee. Let's go play monster.

For Bill, Rick, and Will you are and will always be my three

muses,

my three faces of Heurka.

Veronica it is your belief in me that

keeps the flesh on my bones- Thank you.

Dave- Thank you for all those dark nights at the Spike.

Without you I couldn't be the Vampire

I am today.

The author sends special thanks to all the writers who helped with their critiques on the Online Writers Workshop.

Also, special thanks to Nancy Sinatra, whose song, "Sugar Town," is referenced.

Any questions or comments? Want more? Go to:

WWW.BARDOBOY.COM

All artwork was produced by Len McCawley.

Cover: The Bardo of Sexual Pleasure

Author page: Dead Baby Bird

Author photo by: Len McCawley

The Poet

On a cold winter morning I go to the Thrift Shop to find a poem. My head has been so empty, not unlike a hollow log that lay fallen on a forest floor. Grounded, motionless, strapped down with a seasonless growth of ivy that never seems to die, never seems alive either. Fungi with dry rot mustiness, various hues of blue, and green, and white, coating the insides, crumbly, clingy. Alone, the quiet forest chatter is dampening the outside world.

The aisles are overrun with brick-a-brack. Stacks of old rooster covered dishes surrounding a relinquished owl collection. Wooden owls, china owls, owl fairy lamps and figurines..."What should we get Aunt Mary for her birthday? How about an owl?" After Aunt Mary's death what was to become of her beloved owl collection?

I pass a wall of shelves, spanning floor to ceiling, filled with coffee mugs. The shelves are packed like a Japanese subway car, just cram'em in boys. Men with hats and white gloves press the passengers into the cars so that the doors will close. The woman stacking the shelves is also wearing white gloves. I watch as she tries to fit a "Worlds Best Grandpa" mug onto the shelf with the others. Where is Grandpa now I wonder, packed into the ground with all the other empty mugs whose drink was gone.

An old woman pushes a shopping cart. She smiles as she tries to fit between the gloved woman and me down the narrow aisle. She is wearing three heavy coats. Her legs so swollen she'd given up on shoe laces, her ankles swell over the tops of her open sneakers. As she tries to pass, a cloud of urine rises, pungent ammonia. I can think of nothing else as the funk envelopes me.

The mug stacker also stops and brings the back of her gloved hand to her nose as she winces. The old woman's cart catches the wall of shelves and becomes entangled, as she pushes and pulls the cart trying to free herself, the wall shakes. The mugs sing out in despair with a klinkity-klank... then, train wreck, earthquake, tsunami. Several mugs are in free fall and then smash on the floor.

The old woman, embarrassed, offers her help by picking up the shards. The gloved woman, obviously shaken, first by olfactory assault, then near death by coffee mug, ...not to mention all for about six dollars an hour pay, graciously stops the old woman and checks that the she is unharmed.

"I'll clean it up, honey. I don't what you to get cut."

The old woman now untangled and again smiling moves on. I decide that I too will move to a less odiferous, safer, aisle myself.

A shoe box with family photos, not far enough removed from time to be appreciated yet, priced at ninety-nine cents, catches my attention. It's held together with yellowed tape at the torn corners. I pick up the box and move to a 1970's spanish mediterranean sofa. The sofa has a gothic carved wood back, arms, and legs. The red velvet cushions are heavily worn, like a partially shaved sheep and stained with hard crusty spots. If it were in better shape I would buy it.

Sitting down with the box I start searching through the photos. Maybe, I can find words for my poem among the pictures. *"Picture words, picture show, word show."*

I gaze upon a square photo. "Kodak" is printed in diagonal lines across the back, a boy in a striped red and white shirt, with his dog, are on the front. Their eyes look frozen in time, happy for a moment at least. *"Wordy word...word seizure,"* next photo same boy, same clothes, now with a hose running towards the camera, so quiet, like a silent movie, corners bent, so alive, yet gone and never coming back.

Another, this one must have been the mother. Curlers in full bloom, cigarette burning in the ashtray, old refrigerator in the background, trying to avoid this photo with her raised hand. She is looking directly into the camera, laughing, it's as if she looking into my eyes. She looks so alive and dead, caught in time as if stuck between this world and the next, unable to come, unable to go...*"Silent movie picture show, her words are like seizures causing an amnesia after the shaking."*

Next photo is a small boy in a wheelchair. Something is familiar about this photo. I look down the aisle, there it is. The wheelchair in the photo is parked in the aisle.

I look at the photo again to be sure. I get up, keeping this photo on top of the pile as I make my way to the chair. It is so small and dense, heavy. Primitive, the green leather seat is stained where the body made contact, darker from life's residue.

My eyes well, not because I'm sad. Really, I don't know why I am so moved. There is an invisible connection, a subtle truth. It's beautiful. I guess that should be the poet's job, to expose the beauty. But, at present I can't. The hollow log still lingers. Another shopper also stops to look at the wheelchair.

"I never saw such a little wheelchair." She comments.

I show her the photo...

"Ummp...you should buy it," she mutters.

"What would I do with a wheelchair?" I ask as I chuckle.

"You could use it as a display and put the photo on it." She

replies, as she moves down the aisle mumbling to herself.

I had already considered buying the chair and the box of pho-

tos with "found art" as my excuse. But, I think, why am I doing

this? Is it for poetry, or am I challenging time? Am I resurrect-

ing past moments to be reassembled, proving, that the people in

the photos were here once, and were real? No poem yet. The

photos will have to do for now. I put them under my coat, leave

a dollar at the unmanned register and depart.

Outside the old woman with swollen feet sits panting on the

store's large window ledge. She is enjoying the cold air and

catching her breath. Her eyes are bright blue, clear and un-

touched by her age, they catch my attention. Luck has it I am up

wind.

"Why are there always seagulls here?" She asks me.

I look up and indeed there are seagulls. She continues, *"I never see them around the other shops... Just here."*

I sit on the ledge and look up to the gray cool sky, the purple clouds pass slowly. Three seagulls rise and dive, their calls are empty sirens that echo through the razor sharp winter air. A bright azure light permeates it all. It is so bright I have to turn away.

We sit listening to the melody. Each call is longer than the last, it's similar to an opera. But, more like a wave with wake, a vibration.

When the last note fades the old woman clutches her hands together and chuckles with enjoyment. I too find it entertaining. It's a free concert; it takes us to that middle place... *"Silent movie picture show, her words are like seizures causing an amnesia after the shaking. Her call to me is like a siren taking me to that middle place that feels like a warm bath that soothes and drowns while limbs flail..."*

"That was nice. Thanks," I say to her as I stand up and leave.

I make my way to the car as the seagulls continue their song. It's as if they're calling me, wanting me to stay. I reach for my keys and open the door of my 69' Charger. Sitting behind the wheel I am overcome; the tears arrive so suddenly that they cause pain in my eyes. My crying is like a painful orgasm.

The sobbing soaks my cheeks, I can taste the salt. My nose is running. My intestines melt and settle in a pool below the level of my navel. My breath stutters with each inhalation. I use my sleeve to mop up my face. Drying my eyes I turn the key and make my way home.

Home is a western Philadelphia suburb, about five miles out-side Center City. The drive home takes me through working class towns. The towns are littered with architecture ranging from aluminum covered victorians, some still single family dwellings, others cut up into multiple apartment units with rust-ing fire escapes, to rows of 1950's plain brick tenements that re-sembled internment camps.

Young suburban pedestrians, lacking sufficient money to be driving, are garbed in Philadelphia ghetto style. Although, only five miles away their style always seems to be about two years behind those of the native Philadelphians.

I find it kind of sexy. Men with baggy pants, oversized coat, skull wool cap. Most have a shaggy thin chin beard, cigarette in tote, and a lateral neck tattoo. Woman have multicolored hair, posterior neck tattoo, hip hugging jeans with rolls of skin topping them off as if they had reverse liposuction, baby carriage, and cigarette.

I am renting in a large 1920's home that had been divided into apartments in Lansdowne, Pennsylvania. As I draw nearer to home the neighborhoods improve. From here I can finish the trip blind folded, having come this way so many times. I switch to automatic pilot. This lets my mind wander, and I enter a fish eye lens tunnel.

The houses become a steady stream of large single family homes with only an occasional bastardized apartment conversion, such as mine. All of the houses are stone and you have to pass twenty houses before you see two that are the same, multiple examples of constructions abound, federal style, spanish mission, tutor, arts and crafts, bungalow.

Towering trees line the street displaying their persistence in time. It was quite the neighborhood in the twenties. Traveling through the tunnel I am insulated as the street, sidewalks, trees, and homes bend around me, attain a peek, and are pinched off out of sight.

I get the sense that there are other travelers and pedestrians, but they might as well be specters. I can't stop now, once in the tunnel it is a one way trip. The tunnel delivers me home. I grab my photos, keys, and head to my second floor apartment. I never did like living on first floors.

The entry hall is on the north side of the house. It's always dark, especially during the winter months. Juggling my keys and the photos I shut the door, making the hall darker. The overhead light is burned out, but the dim glow from the second floor's wall sconces help a bit. The mailboxes and open staircase are on the right.

Fuck! My mailbox is open again. How many times does that make this week? No mail. Maybe one of the other tenants slipped it under my door. I close the box, turn around, put the key into my apartment lock. This is when vertigo hits. The floor under my left leg rises three feet while the right falls two feet.

I reach out for the wall with my free hand to steady myself as my feet dance trying to find level ground. I miss the wall and catch the sconce's exposed light bulb as it explodes with a loud pop and shower of glass.

Suddenly, I realize that I don't remember climbing the stairs. *"Silent movie picture show, her words are like seizures causing an amnesia after the shaking. Her call to me is like a siren taking me to that middle place that feels like a warm bath that sooth and drown while limbs flail. The invited bitterness that stings my tongue, holds my breath, and fills my eyes with a black rainbow ooze..."* Raging sea becomes a still pond. I steady myself and look at my fingers. No cuts. *"Lucky."* I open my door. No mail here either.

Inside, "Home again, home again, jiggidy jig..." This quote often comes to mind when I get home. It's a line spoken by Kaiser, the toy, in Blade Runner when Sebastian enters his apartment. *"Home again, home again..."* I say, as the last bit of Mr. Vertigo leaves me.

I take a deep breath and take a deep look, one large room cut in two by a counter top. Small parlor - bedroom with a open messy futon bed, smaller kitchen, a bathroom off the kitchen.

Two large windows span the wall across from where I stand. They are the only windows this unit has. When the windows are not covered with purple and brown batik curtains, I look out onto trees that are occasionally clad in plastic shopping bags that have escaped their destiny only to be caught by the deciduous beings, telephone wires, sometimes blue sky with clouds, birds, squirrels, and sometimes a neighborhood boy playing squirrel, or spy.

Homegrown art decorates the disheveled white plaster walls along with water stains. Some of the art was found in the trash, or given to me by friends for good deeds done, others bought at the Thrift Shop. My apartment faces east, pretty bright in the morning. Sunrises were so much more enjoyable than sunsets. Lately, sunsets have been more soothing.

I set my box of photos on the counter top and toss my keys into the metal swastika ashtray. I am trying to resurrect my poetry. New poems are evading me and I haven't been able to find my old poems.

I should go through more of the photos, do some word hunting, but I'm tired now. I make my way to my bed through the small piles of mags and tattered paperback books. I lay on my back with one hand on my groin. Staring up, the tin ceiling is so detailed. The stamped patterns in this shadowy light look like figures depicting an old story, an ancient battle between heaven and hell. This bed feels so good. It takes just a moment and I'm asleep.

The dreams arrive. Silent movie picture show...Old fat smelly woman panting, eyes of a baby, bright and azure blue. Laughing. WHAT... IS... THAT... SMELL? ...her words are like seizures... young sinewy man, blond, in shape, tattoo, half naked, sweating convulsing. Mumbling schizophrenic pushing a cart, ...causing an amnesia after the shaking. CHRIST... DID... A... COW...

SHIT... IN... HERE? Her call to me is like a siren... "Why are

there seagulls always here?"

A handsome Philly style man and his girl date try to make me

rise from the dance floor while disco lights flash bright white.

The floor is packed with dancers entranced by the hard rock mu-

sic.

"GET UP! GET UP!" They demand, shouting over the mu-

sic.

I open my eyes and see the two hovering over me. The disco

lights are glaring, but I can still make out their handsome faces,

they appear happy to see me awake. *"Do I know you?"* I ask.

They look at each other and laugh.

"Come on man...your doin fine. Let's go."

They pull me up and lead me off the dance floor towards a glowing light at the end of the bar. The light is suffocating and numbs my mind. *I have to get out of here.* I brake away from them, burying myself into the crowd of dancers. The bar becomes a maze and I'm lost.

While searching for an exit I come upon young men seated on a row of stools. They are young skateboard dudes surrounded by a soft smokey radiance, each is holding a skateboard and bopping to the music.

Each dude is physically deformed, pointed teeth, or shrunken mouth. One has an enormous left arm with a tiny right arm. Another guy has one ear near his temple, almost on top of his head, the other ear is dangling from his jaw.

"Nice head," I think to myself.

Their haircuts are styled to look messy. They aren't frightening, just odd. They notice me starring at them and shoot me a smile. One yells out to me, *"Really cool place, huh?"* I smile

back and nod yes; I feel comfortable with them in my daze.

The handsome couple are cutting their way through the danc-

ers, coming for me again. There is an exit on the other side of

the dance floor, as I make my way for it I become tangled in the

crowd.

Another man, a handsome blond smoking a cigarette, who

seems to know me, yells out in a creepy German accent, " Don't

trust them, that fat smelly hag, ...or pretty faces, or any of them.

They are all CRA-ZEEE."

I jolt awake, freezing. My futon is soaked with sweat, the

room is black. Memories of my dream replay while I retrieve

my blanket. I curl up and fall back to sleep.

Brightness creeps across my walls like a sundial without

markings. There weren't anymore dreams last night. Just good

sleep. A dark place. Dark not because it is bad or devoid of

light, but because it is a place without memories. I get up and

head for the fridge. Not much inside. I pull out an open tin can

of tomato juice. The triangle openings are rusted, fuck it. I pour a glass and take in a gulp. *Would be better with some vodka.*

Swallowing the juice brings on the instant need to pee. I head to

the bathroom.

Standing in front of the bowl with cock in hand, my pissing

seems eternal. Leaning over to my right I look at myself in the

mirror while I pee. Blond hair hangs to my dark brows. My

blue eyes look old for thirty-three.

I remember looking into my eyes as a child for what felt like

hours. In some way I knew they would change, as if, someday I

would be looking at someone else. Over the years I would visit

the mirror, again and again, to see if I could see that same child,

trying to keep the youth from leaving, even if my eyes had

changed.

There's something about rituals that keep us the same, or

temporarily exposes the "real" us. I think about the people in the

photos and their eyes trapped in time. Finally, the piss is over. I

wash up in the sink. I leave the bathroom and look around my

my apartment, *"Where the fuck would I put a 70's spanish medi-*

terranean sofa?"

I grab my tomato juice and a stool by the end of the counter and sit down. I reach for the box of photos and slide them down to me. The wheelchair boy is still on top, along with the mom, and the boy with striped shirt. I look into their motionless eyes again before going through more pictures.

There are wads of company snapshots, men with 1950's thick brim glasses, and buzz cuts, all are gathered behind a round table draped with a white sheet. A company logo statue sits in the center of the table along with company products...boring.

I come across another grouping of photos held together with a deteriorating rubber band labeled, "1968 shore vacation." The rubber band snaps as I remove it. The stack of photos flies from my hands, snapshots stream across the room. Sandy waves with bright sunshine, plastic disposable sunglasses, smiling faces in muscle poses are littering my room.

I crawl across a sand dune on my futon, making a right by the the pail and slide over the edge to the sandy floor hunting for the remainder of the photos. Sand crabs sing a cricket song while I make my way on all fours across empty tampon wrappers and cigarette butts.

Up through the sand a hugh phallus grows before me. It's made of drift wood and is tethered with a rope. On my knees before it, scintillating yellow sun in my eyes, I pause because of the brightness.

A strong gust of wind blows and a seagull's silhouette lands on the meatus. Its soft blue light blocks the sunshine. I close my eyes against the blowing sand. When I open my eyes the beach is gone and I'm holding several photos.

The pictures are more than moving, they're transforming. *Maybe, the Thrift Shop has more of this family's story and my poem.* I leave the box on the bed. I grab my coat, smell my armpit, ...not too bad, and head back to the Thrift Shop with a hand full of the Kodaks.

While driving I think about the poem I'm working on, Silent Movie Picture Show. I should start writing it down. No matter how many times I repeat it, and believe I won't forget any of the words, my recent experiences with memory shows me otherwise.

When I start to repeat the lines of the poem out loud, until I can get paper and pen, a fowl odor engulfs the interior of my car. I wonder, did I leave a half eaten lunch in here? The smell intensifies.

What is it? I sniffed the air trying to make out the scent... sweat from an alcoholic after a week long binge? No... Can of cat food forgotten in the fridge for a month? Close, but no. French onion soup? Definitely soupy. I retest one of my underarms. *"God. It is my own B-O! Christ."*

I make a quick detour to the Dollar Dollar store to grab a stick of cheap deodorant and some soap. I could wash up in the bathroom at the Thrift Shop, I have seen many a homeless man and woman do the same. There is a Dollar Dollar on the way.

I walk into Dollar Dollar, passing the gum ball machines on my left. Helium tanks with floating silver balloons are on my right. Muzak is playing overhead. "...she doesn't mind the time, she doesn't mind the flow...she's here to take you...if you'll go..." I never heard that tune done in over head shopping music before, it's sort of cool.

The center of the store holds the cash register along with a long line of people trailing to the back. The check out line reminds me of a dragon's tail. Standing in front of the line at the register is an old woman dressed completely in red. Her skin is white. She is wearing a red Three Musketeer style hat, with a large red feather on the side. Her eyelids are painted with bright red glitter, lips vibrant ruby red, red shirt, red jacket, red coat... fingernails... red, looks like the old biddy took advantage of those after Valentine's day sales.

She's purchasing a seagull. It's made of resin, it hovers over a quartz stone base with a metal wire. Watching it sway takes me out of the moment. 1968 vacation, sandy waves, not coming, not going, but always in motion. When I look up she is looking back at me with a penetrating gaze. Embarrassed, I turn my eyes and continue my deodorant search.

Wandering through the store I come upon the shelves holding the seagulls, there must be a hundred of them, all wobbling. I pick up one and shake it back and forth when there is a loud pop and feedback buzz. The music stops and an announcement starts in a threatening tin man voice, "*I warned you. Stay away from them. All of them. Meet me in the back if you want to make it out in one piece. It's not too late boy.*"

I set the figurine down and look around. No one else in the store seems to think the announcement is out of place. It's as if I'm the only one who hears it.

Curious, I head to the back of the store and find a door that's ajar, coming from behind it is a dull yellow mist. It's relaxing and rejuvenating. I want to enter it, but before I can reach the door the red lady moves into my path. She is pissed. Red-orange flames surge from her now enormous nostrils. A glistening red snake rises up from under her red dress and snaps at me.

"Some fucking Valentine's sale lady." I yell, as I fall backwards taking a couple shelves down with me.

I tear out of the store. The shoppers all crouch down, as if a terrorist bomb exploded.

"What was that?" Several customers ask.

"It must have been the wind. The back door blew open before the shelves fell."

"Jesus," exclaims another shopper, grabbing her chest with open hand, as the store attendants make their way to clean up the mess.

Running like a frighten cat, without thought of consequence of where my feet may take me, I bolt around the corner and stop behind a trash bin. Squatting, holding my head, I catch my breath. *"What the fuck is going on? I must be loosing my fucking mind! What the fuck was that?"*

I'm used to my daydreams, they're often an inspiration for my writing. But, this? It seems so fucking real. I pull the Kodak photos from my coat pocket. These have something to do with what's going on. I get up, looking over my shoulder, still shaken, I go back to my car and back to the Thrift Shop.

I stand for a moment in front of the Thrift Shop door. *"Next stop furniture, knickknacks, odds and ends, children's wheel-chairs, and discarded family memories."*

Time slows as I push open the door. The air is like an invisible molasses and presses against the door as I try to enter. Using all my strength I am able to open the door enough to squeeze through. When the door snaps shut behind me the atmosphere clears and time resumes its normal flow.

The Thrift Shop is vacant except for me. The dim light gives art and advertisements the appearance of sacred carvings covering the walls. Stale air lingers around racks of old clothes, shoes, record albums, and piles of dusty used furniture, along with household items. The four walls seem more solid as they seal the contents in. I hear a rhythm echoing from the walls, its tune repeating itself over and over like the scratch and pop of a needle stuck at the end record album. The reverberations make it hard to locate the source of this sound, as it gets louder I turn to my right.

Coming towards me down one of the aisles is the green wheelchair. It's slowly rolling, the wheels squeaking with each turn. It is luminous, casting a blinding green aura on all things it passes. As it gets closer the green light grows more intense.

I can hear someone calling me from the green light. The sound of the voice shakes me like a rattle with each syllable spoken. As the chair gets nearer, the voice grows louder, and my body begins to disintegrate, head separates from neck, wrists from arms, feet from legs. Skin then separates from muscle, and muscle moves away from bone. While the voice pounds at me I realize that I am going away, I'm loosing myself. Each consonant uttered pauses my heart and steals my breath. There is no more after this.

I remember as a boy, burning the abdomen of a restrained moth with a lit punk, when the realization of what I had done came to light I wanted to reverse time and make it right again for the moth. But, I couldn't go back, I couldn't fix it. If I let go now there will be no fix for this.

"What the fuck. What the fuck is going on?" I scream.

I pull myself together and move away from the light. It's as if the coming apart is a dream, I'm whole again. I make my way to the exit. But, the door is sealed, fastened by time itself, frozen. I run for the back of the store. There are double doors that are used for accepting donations. It appears to be the only other way out. I bolt towards my new exit and throw all my weight against the double doors. They give way easily. Too easily. Shit!

There is a slight sensation of spinning slowly, more like drifting. I try to open my eyes and then realize they are open. I am surrounded by blackness. I can't see my hands or legs, but I can touch them, this lets me know that they are there and not disintegrated. I touch my face, I feel my breath leave my nostrils. It is relaxing and soothing. It is like being in the middle of the ocean during a new moon, pitch black, naked, floating.

I wave my arms and legs about, trying to propel myself, searching for the edge, if there is one, when I glimpse a radiant spinning object heading my way. It is very small, but gradually becomes larger. It stops about a foot away from my face. It's a paper box, torn corners with yellowed tape holding it together.

"The box of photos I left on the futon?"

A photo rises from the box and presents itself to me. It's the boy in the striped shirt with his dog. Tears flood my eyes, while my stomach tumbles in the weightlessness. *"Paul. It's my brother Paul and Derry."*

Another photo rises from the box. *"Mom."* I say out loud, fully sobbing. Not someone else's mom, but my mom. I remember her Saturday night Jean Nate baths, followed by hair curlers. I can smell the lemons.

I reach for the two photos and they vanish. The next photo comes; It's the boy in the wheelchair. *"Paul after the accident..."* It was a beautiful day. The sky was clear and the sun shined so brightly. Dad had been away working in another state on a "good paying" job. Paul, as always, is with Derry in the yard.

Mom had just hung a load of laundry. Sheets, pillow cases, jeans and shirts blew on the clothesline like Tibetan prayer flags. The large rusted metal door that lead to the basement washing machine stood open. She sat on an aluminum yard chair with wide plastic green and white weavings. She was painting her toenails, half crouched with her heel on the edge of the seat.

Her white and gold combo radio-alarm clock was plugged into the outlet next to her chair. Nancy Sinatra's Sugar Town was playing. I was lying in the grass drawing in my pad, practicing perfect circles. Derry caught site of a rabbit and took after it. Paul followed, both heading toward the road.

Mom must have known this was not good. She dropped the bottle of nail polish and joined the chase. I dodged after them. A large roar filled the air. Two boys on dirt bikes headed toward us.

By the time mom made it to the edge of the road, Paul was already restraining Derry in the middle of the road, when one of the bikes hit them both. Silence, quiet, except for the radio playing Sugar Town.

The boy on the bike flew and hit a tree. It killed him instantly. The other bike stopped and spun to face the trauma. Derry tumbled within a cloud of dust and dirt, also killed instantly. Paul tumbled behind Derry. When he came to rest he laid crumpled in the road. Mom stood aghast, unable to move. This was the beginning of her suffering. She was never the same since that day.

The remainder of Paul's life was occupied with surgeries and complications from surgery. He lived for about two more years, sentenced to live it in a wheelchair. My life was relegated to the shadows. From that day on my existence seemed to take place on the edge of reality. Paul was the focus of the family since the accident, even after his death a cloud of depression masked my life. Mom died several years later. She just let everything go. She took part of my dad with her.

Trembling from this picture show and the deluge of memories, my gaze stays fixed on the box as another photo presents itself. This is a new photo. It wasn't in box with the others, but it also shows a scene from the past. It's me when I found the letter from my love Drew after he'd taken his own life. We'd spent almost every moment of our adolescent and adult lives with each other. Living together, or at times separate, mostly separate when Drew's drinking would get heavy.

He would always tell the same story. The tale of Drew and I, when he first saw me in the hallway in high school. He'd said he knew from that day we would be together. Over the years we would argue over who saw who first...

Another new photo. Me, after my suicide, bloated in a bath tub, my eyes black and still. A bar of soap, a present given to me from Drew, shaped into a seagull dangles from the faucet above my swollen head.

Silent movie picture show,

her words are like seizures causing an amnesia

after the shaking.

Her call to me is like a siren taking me to that middle place

that feels like a warm bath that soothes and drowns

while limbs flail.

The poison is not repulsive but familiar, natural.

I lose track of where it ends and I begin. It is all me!

The invited bitterness holds my breath,

and fills my eyes with a black rainbow ooze,

while warm slippery water fills my lungs

Setting free old familiars,

rejoicing in my re-acquaintance like two dogs in heat,

I take the drink back and everything is gone!

The Wakker

You are now at 10th and Cherry streets, in the kitchen of a Philadelphia Chinatown apartment. The room is tiny. The appliances are old and noisy. A tasseled chinese paper lantern covers the ceiling light, men with rickshaws transport beautiful white faced women with umbrellas. The window is draped with lacy white curtains with red trim. Bus engines, sirens, and car horns occasional rise from the street entering the window and then leave like a lost fly.

It's a beautiful day. A breeze plays with the window curtains and paper lantern tassel. Seated at a small table near the window are a grandfather with his grandson.

The grandfather was born in China and has been living in Philadelphia for the past thirty-three years. His grandson is visiting. They're having a solemn conversation after attending a belated funeral service. The deceased was the son of a family friend and coworker who took his own life months ago.

On the window ledge is a small altar with a Wakker figurine depicting Heruka, a human-beast with four faces and twelve extended arms.

Each face represents the four directions of this world and twelve arms represent the twelve dimensions of reality. Heruka's faces radiate perfect happiness. A lotus shaped porcelain dish filled with red water sits in front of the figurine. A blood offering.

"Ye Ye, why did your friend kill himself?" The boy asks.

"Nobody will ever know for sure. He was very sad."

"I get sad too, but I wouldn't ever kill myself. I would miss you too much."

The grandfather chuckles at this statement, *" I hope you wouldn't because I would also miss you. Just as everybody can get a cold, not everybody will die from it. Everybody will occa-*

sionally get sad. Sadness is part of life, like getting a cold.

Some will die from the sadness, but most people get over the

sadness like a bad cold."

The boy continues, *"Ye Ye, where do we go when we die?"*

"Well, people believe different things about what happens af-

ter death."

"What do you believe Ye Ye?"

Still smiling the grandfather says, *"I believe what the Wakker*

taught."

In a rush to align himself with his grandfather the boy blurts

out, *"I believe that too."* He doesn't really understand and im-

mediately asks, *"What did Wakker teach?"*

The grandfather collects his thoughts, *"The Wakker taught that life is an endless cycle, everything you do has an affect on everything else, eventually your actions return to you, good and bad."*

The boy listens intently, then asks, *"So we should try to do only good things?"*

Smiling, the grandfather replies, *"You should try to break the cycle, the best thing to do is to get away from the good and the bad."*

The boy looks at his grandfather, puzzled. The Grandfather continues, *"The Wakker teaches us that we are all made to relive our lives over and over again. The good and bad deeds return to us causing more actions and reactions. More good things can lead to more bad things. On and on it goes.*

It is like being given a test over and over again until you get a perfect score. Each time you take the test you learn a little more, but each time your are given the test there is a chance you may do worse."

A flash of understanding appears on the boy's face, " *I saw a movie once where a man kept living the same day over and over again, he was trapped. How do we get out of the trap Ye Ye?"*

The grandfather answers, *"First you have to know you are trapped. The hardest prison to escape from is the one that you don't even know you are in.*

In Wakkism we call this prison a Bardo, it is the place in between other places. Sometimes, it can be very subtle, or like a sweet dream. Other times it can be a very bad nightmare. Remember, don't be fooled by the sweet dream, even when it is beautiful it is still a prison, because it is not real."

The grandfather gets up from his seat across from the boy and leaves the room. When he returns he has a book in his hand and squeezes into a chair next to the boy, *"Our best chance of becoming free from repeating our lives and entering the Bliss State, Heaven, is during our present life time. We accomplish this by becoming awake through the practice of Wakkism. If we do not succeed while we are alive we get several chances after each death."*

"Isn't living again and again good Ye Ye? We could see each other again and again."

"It would appear so, but if you mess up during that lifetime you may come back as a sick person suffering everyday, or as a dog living in the streets, or even as a bug in the ground. It is best to enter the Bliss State and avoid more lifetimes. Only in Bliss will you find true happiness."

"Where is Bliss Ye Ye?"

The Grandfather takes a short pause and collects his thoughts, *"The Wakker tells us that the Bliss State can be any-where. It can even be right in front of you. There are two reason why we can't see it, or experience it. The first reason is our sleeping minds. The second reason is the Great Faker. Together our sleeping minds and the Great Fakers hold us prisoner here in life and later in the bardos."*

The Grandfather holding The Book of Bardo goes on with the lesson, *"This is the instruction manuel for people when they die. The lessons learned by this book during a person's life will help them in death."*

He opens the book. While reading he rewords the lesson best as he can, so his grandson can understand.

"On the first day after death the great Blue Wakker will come to the person with a bright azure blue light. If the person sees the light as their own soul they will not be afraid and will merge

with the light and enter the Bliss State. If the persons eyes are

blocked by illusion or the Great Faker they will become fright-

ened of the brilliance and avoid the light.

A second light will appear, a dull white light that will be

tempting. The dead person must avoid the dull light as this will

lead to a rebirth. They will be reborn in the god realm. In the

god realm life is long and there are many pleasures, but these are

all illusions and are only temporary.

Death even comes to those in the god realm. With death

comes the risks of rebirth. All of these visions by the deceased

are just projections of the dead persons mind. The visions are

bare truth, but are cloaked by illusions."

The boy sits staring at his grandfather, puzzled. The grandfather, seeing the boy's confusion, continues the lesson in more
detail.

"The Wakker with bright light represent the persons true na-

ture. Every person gets a glimpse of their true self after death.

Hopefully, they will recognize it as their true mind, their soul, so they can merge with the light and enter the Bliss State. The light is the "real" person stripped of the bardos, the prisons, and the false sense of self known as the Great Faker.

The Great Faker is like the jail keeper in the bardos. It will tell you what it thinks is good and bad. It tells you what makes you happy and sad, thus keeping you lost.

The Great Faker keeps the person in a drugged like state with illusions and temptations. The Great Faker is created with each birth. Every person is born with their own Great Faker. Even in death, the Great Faker is present and clings to the person. It will try to sabotage the merging with the light and interfere with the deceased entering the Bliss State."

"Why does the Great Faker do this?"

"Because the Great Faker is not real. Its existence depends on the illusions continuing. The belief in our illusions give the Great Faker life. We sustain it by staying asleep, thus avoiding

our true nature. When a person enters the Bliss State the Great Faker can no longer exist. It is very smart and tricky. It will even tell you it wants you to be free, to go to bliss. It will tell you it is only here for your happiness, but all along it will lead you away from true bliss."

...Outside the old woman with swollen feet sits panting on the store's large window ledge. She is enjoying the cold air and catching her breath. Her eyes are bright blue, clear and un-touched by her age, they catch my attention. Luck has it I am up wind.

"Why are there always seagulls here?" She asks me. I look up and indeed there are seagulls. She continues, *"I never see them around the other shops...just here."* I sit on the ledge and look up to the gray cool sky, the purple clouds pass slowly. A bright azure light permeates it all. It is so bright I have to turn away...

"On the second day another great Wakker, along with his wife, will appear out of a brilliant white light and offer enlightenment to the deceased. If the person recognizes the light they will not be afraid and will merge with the light and enter the Bliss State. If not, they will become frightened of the brilliance and avoid the light.

A second light will also appear, a smokey white light, that will be tempting. The dead person must avoid the dull light as this will lead to a rebirth into one of the hell realms. It will be a place of constant suffering, although not permanent, it is hard to reach the Bliss State from the hell realms. It could be here on earth as life as a slug, or in Hell itself with other tormented beings. Again, the Great Faker will always interfere."

... A handsome Philly style man and his girl date try to make me rise from the dance floor while disco lights flash bright white... They pull me up and lead me off the dance floor towards a glowing light at the end of the bar. The light is suffocating and numbs my mind. *I have to get out of here...*

"On the third day after death the blessed Yellow Wakker will appear out of a brilliant light and offer enlightenment to the deceased. If the person can recognize the brilliance they will not be afraid and will merge with it, entering the Bliss State. If they do not see the light as their own mind, they will become frightened of the brilliance and avoid it.

A second light will also appear, a soft blue light that will be tempting. The dead person must avoid the dull light as this will lead to a rebirth into the human realm. In the human realm the person is cursed to be born, grow old, become sick and die. There are pleasures in the human realm, but they are illusions and are not true happiness. The pleasures are only temporary."

... Up through the sand a hugh phallus grows before me. It's made of drift wood and is tethered with a rope. On my knees before it, scintillating yellow sun in my eyes, I pause because of the brightness.

A strong gust of wind blows and a seagull's silhouette lands on the meatus. Its soft blue light blocks the sunshine. I close my eyes against the blowing sand. When I open my eyes the beach is gone...

"On the fourth day after death the Red Wakker will appear and offer enlightenment to the deceased. If the person can see this light as being their soul, they will not be afraid, merge with the light and enter the Bliss State. If the person is fearful, they will avoid the red light.

A second soft yellow light will emerge. This dull light will be tempting to the deceased, but they must avoid this light. It leads to a rebirth in the realm of the insatiable. In this realm beings are fat and are always hungry. They are given tiny mouths, so they can't fit all the food that is set out before them. Those who are reborn there can never be satisfied."

...Standing in front of the line at the register is an old woman dressed completely in red. Her skin is white. She is wearing a red, Three Musketeer style, hat with a large red feather on the side. Her eyelids are painted with bright red glitter, lips vibrant

ruby red, red shirt, red jacket, red coat... fingernails... red...

"On the fifth day of death the blessed Green Wakker, will ap-

pear to the deceased and offer enlightenment. Again, If the per-

son recognizes the light they will not be afraid and merge with

the brilliant green light. They will enter the Bliss State. If the

person has fear, they will move away from it. At this same point

a soft red light will appear, but they must avoid it.

The dim red light leads to a rebirth in the realm of the half

gods. The half gods are warlike. Their lives are filled with fight-

ing and killing. These beings are paranoid and violent. They

think all other beings are their enemies. All matter in their

world is viewed as a weapon.

A cool stream in hot summer, while seen as a refreshing bath

or cool drink to us, to a half god it is to be used to drown or boil

their enemies. In the Bliss State the stream is just a stream. It is

neither good or bad. The stream's beauty is contained in its true nature... It is just a stream.   It is very difficult for the half gods to see the simple stream."

...Coming towards me down one of the aisles is the green wheelchair. It is luminous, casting a blinding green aura on all things it passes. It is slowly rolling, its wheels squeaking with each turn. As it gets closer the green light grows more intense...

"So we only have five days after death Ye Ye?" The grandson asks, trying to make sense of it all.

"Five days here can be years or hours in the Bardos. Time is only used as a rough guide."

The boy looks confused. The grandfather continues. *"When you are playing a fun game doesn't it feel like time goes by quickly? Hours go by, but it feels like minutes and before you know it your mother is calling you in for dinner. On the other hand, when you get a needle at the doctor's office doesn't it feel like time is dragging? It only takes seconds, but it feels like*

hours."

The boy flashes a smile of understanding.

INTER-BARDO LOG #1

Hello there... HEL-LOW! Do you not speak when spoken to? HEY YOU! Reader. Yes, you. I am addressing you now. We are taking a break from the story. I wanted to visit your world, since you have been to mine. It's only fair. You can close your book or try to shut me off, but I'll be here when you return. I will look in while you dream at night.

My seed is already in you and it is growing. It's impossible to un-read, to un-know, what was put inside you. I'm in your head right now. Hello. See, you hear me in your mind. Each word read or heard implants me into your world. I am among the synapses in your brain becoming real flesh and blood.

I exist first as a word on a page, then I am transmitted by light or sound. I enter through the eyes, ears, and mind as an electric impulse. This physically changes your brain forever, I become one of your memories.

Even years from now, when I am seemingly forgotten, I will be in you. Even after your death, as your cold body lies in the ground, I will exist in the folds of your brain.

You're wondering who I am? I go by many names, but for now you can call me Book. As you read I grow. Already, I can smell you. I can almost touch you. But, I am not yet solid enough to move from the confinement of your mind. You must journey on. The more you take me in, the more durable I become.

I have the Chinese man and grandson, along with the poet Bardo Boy, bound and gagged at the moment. I am not speaking literally, of course. I got tired of the old man's Blah Blah Blah. I remove them from their reality, they will have no memory of their temporary removal. I hold them prisoner, each in their own cell. It's easy. You see, they all believe they are real, each with a life of their own. They have no idea of the reality that lies above them, your world. As long as they believe this they remain my captives. Maybe, out of all of them, the Chinese Wakkist has an understanding of alternate existences. But, enough of this for now.

I am going to speed things up a bit for you, sweetie, deepening my place in your mind. Bardo Boy is floating in the restored memory of his suicide and recent life. The mother of the Chinese boy arrives at her father's apartment to take her son home. This gives the old Chinese man time alone. He is preparing for the practice of One. Wakkists do One for the dead, to help them navigate the bardos. He is trying to send Bardo Boy to the Bliss State. But, he will not succeed while I am in control.

That's it for now. While I retreat to the back of your mind for a nap, the story will unravel. In the meantime think about this, death is nothing more than casting off our old bodies like worn out clothes, it can be a great opportunity and source of power even without the Bliss State. Who needs bliss when you have me!

END INTER-BARDO LOG #1

Bardo Boy

A bloated naked body is submerged in a bathtub. Face up, its eyes are blackened with death. The skin is soft and loose, about to come away from the bone. Shit expelled at the time of death is now completely dissolved giving the water a stagnant, pond scum, quality.

Fumes rise from the water and fill the tiny bathroom with an odor that could cause instant spewing. It smells like shit mixed with burnt hair. Flies teem on the window and bathtub, lapping up the encrusted scum that is caked on the sides.

Next to the tub, on the black and white tile floor, are pointy green pods. They hang lip on stems with green pointy leaves. Datura Stramonium, jimson, a hallucinogen that can be found in any backyard. Taken to experience euphoria, in large doses it causes confusion, delirium, seizure, and death.

The bathroom is quiet. The death water is completely still, as if frozen. Suddenly, tumefied skin begins to tighten. The black rainbow ooze that was covering the eyes retracts under the eyelids, like a slug retreating from salt. Pupils constrict. Eyes blink and flash with consciousness. Shit water whirlpools, as it swirls it cleanses itself of pollutants. I rise from the bath. Sitting up, I puke the soapy liquid from my lungs. Winds streaming from the east, west, north, and south force their way through my nose and mouth, inflating my body.

I cover my face with open palms as I breath. I exhale into my cupped hands before taking my air back in through my broad nose. I feel my lips, warm and full. I move my hands away from my face. I study my body, it's solid and strong. Water drains from my hair and runs over my biceps. Small streams trail down from my shoulders over my erect nipples and abdo-men. Looking down into the bath I see my dark pubic hair wave under the surface of the water. My cock thick and buoyant rests on my balls. My feet, *what the fuck,* toenails that look like claws.

I look at my hands again. My fingernails are similar. They look like human nails, but are white and tapered at the ends. I tap them on the tub, they're hard and metallic. I swat the inside of the tub like a tiger. My nails enter the cast iron as if it's tin foil. Water drains from the slashed openings.

I step out of the tub to check-out myself in the mirror. Parts of the silver backing has dulled in a stamped sponged pattern. I peer at myself through the areas that are still reflective, my face is only partially visible because of the mirror's defects. Moving my head back and forth, I am able to piece myself together.

My hair is black like tar, glistening from the wetness of my death bath. It is as straight as straw and thick. It comes to the tips of my ears. My eyebrows are also dark and dense. My eyes remain blue.

Moving closer to the mirror I look deeper into my eyes. Pupils reacting swiftly, as if they are a machine downloading volumes of information. I wonder if these are the eyes I looked into when I was a child. In death I am continuing the same mirror ritual I did in life, looking deeply into my eyes trying to see who is behind them.

My memory is restored. My life and death lay before me, but where am I now? *Is this Hell?* If it is Hell it's not too bad. I feel pretty good, for a dead guy. Leaning against the sink looking

into my distorted reflection I think of Drew and whisper his

name. I sense that he is here too. I have to find him. A poem I

wrote after his death returns to me.

You know what I did after you died?

I rounded up all your straws,

the long ones, you used to reach all the way to the bottom

of the Absolute bottle,

that was after you stopped using glasses, ice cubes, and mixes.

I filled all those straws with cement,

and when they were hard

I sharpened each one to a spear like point.

I implanted them in the dirt above you,

each 1/2 inch from the other.

When I was done and your grave blanketed

by a multitude of tiny obelisks pointing to the sky,

I laid upon them, and

I sobbed and sobbed.

I move away from the sink, I'm hammered with burning pain. The air in immediate contact with my skin has become a vapory acid. My skin simmers and smokes. *"Has Hell begun, my punishment for suicide?"* The pain is searing and I cannot move. The pain removes me from the moment, time is meaningless, all other sensations and thoughts cease. My head reals back, damp hair steams as I bellow.

The surface of my skin, first melted, solidifies. The pain retreats. What was skin is now a tenebrous leather. I am clad in boots, pants, and open biker jacket. The fit is like... wearing my own skin. The boots rise up to just bellow the bend in my knee, they are fastened with several pewter skull studs running up along the outside, enclosing the bottom length of my pants.

Two thick pewter chains, cast in the likeness of bones, encircle my ankles. The pants stop just above my pubic bone, about three inches below my navel. I turn to look at my backside in the mirror. The jacket ends just above my ass.

There is a pattern carved into the leather occupying the entire back of the jacket. It's hard to make out the image with this aged mirror. I remove the jacket to look at the back. The marking depicts a large man-beast with four faces, and twelve arms.

The faces are gruesome with large saber teeth and sneering expressions. Each head is wearing a crown of human skulls. I study the carving more intently. There is an object in each hand, lasso, severed head, trident... One hand is holding a bowl made from a human skull, it is filled to the brim with liquid. *"Blood. Heruka, The Blood Drinker. The most powerful Wakkened being."* I murmur. *But, I thought Heruka was only a myth?*

I clutch the jacket to my face and breath in the leather, trying to compose myself. Drew comes to my mind again. I feel he is here, wherever *here* is. So far it isn't Heaven and ain't exactly Hell either. I have to find him. I throw on my jacket, as I leave the bathroom I pause to look out onto my living room.

Same apartment, yet changed. It is neat and clean, surgical. Everything has been removed. The windows, furniture, and remnants of my life are gone. The room is naked. The illumination filling the room is being generated from every surface. Walls, floor, and ceiling have become glowing white glass.

There is a large rectangular glass slab just off center of the room. It is just large enough to hold one body. The slab is also glowing white.

I enter the room as a loud ringing explodes in my head, it rattles my eyes, my ears follow with a deafening reverberation. I step backwards from the white room into the bathroom.

While overcome by this buzz I notice a chain hanging from the tub's faucet. It's where the seagull rope soap had been, a present to me from Drew in life. I had hung it from the faucet before taking the jimson weed. It has become a pewter chain with pewter seagull charm. Kneeling next to the tub I unhook the chain from the faucet, stars of light reflect from my fingernails as I roll the chain between my fingers. This dampens the clamor in my brain. I place the charm around my neck. The resonant sound that is bombarding my head stops.

I stand to leave and I feel a gnawing in my stomach. It's not a pain or discomfort, more an emptiness that needs to be filled. My skin tingles as its sensitivity has increased. I can feel the movement of every molecule touching me as the atmosphere rolls over my skin and moves away. I touch myself, feeling the muscles of my belly, this starts a cascade of enjoyable shivers over my body, the ripples enter my groin, pass around to my anus and travel up my back causing tiny electrical burst at my neck. My lips and penis are pumping with warm blood, there isn't a full erection, just a pleasant fullness pushing against my pants.

I can see the entire room as if I'm everywhere. I hear the bugs in the bathroom wall and the creaking of the peeling paint. I smell warm salty iron, its aroma brings the sensation of that gnawing emptiness to the front of my experience. I want to slip into the scent.

Breathing heavy, I enter the white room again. I'm enveloped in an invisible metallic cloud. I hear the rhythm of two heart beats. One just a moment out of sync with the other.

The dancing sound cradles my ears, it adds to the cascade of pleasure coursing through my body, spreading across my belly and chest.

I draw the intoxicating cloud deep into my lungs. I linger in the sound and smell, enjoying the passion. My penis is pressing harder against my pants. *"Maybe, this is Heaven."* I say, my voice two octaves lower. A door opens in one of the glowing panels. Two beings enter. I can't see them or into the hall behind them, it's flooded with light. They are silhouettes at present.

When the door seals behind them, the brightness retracts and I see them. Two tall black women stand across from me. The glowing slab separates us. Each is a twin to the other. They are wearing a sparkling silver garb that fits them tightly. It's as if it's their own skin. Their feet and lower legs are encased in silver glamour rock platform boots.

The only exposed skin is from their necks and up, that's where I can see their pulse. This gives me a full erection. I breath in the salty, metal, iron scent that is filling the room, it's emanating from them. My chest heaves with each breath. My eyes take in their short cropped afros and large firm breasts. Their faces are soft and round. They have wide eyes and sharp, lucent, canine teeth. White crystalline smiles.

This is so fucking good. Nothing to do, nowhere to be, thoughtless. Warm streams of iron pulse through their veins with each beat of their hearts. One of the women moves to the slab and lies supine with her head bending backwards over the edge exposing her neck. *An offering to me?* The other, moving like a breeze, straddles me from behind.

My clothes smoke and retreat, becoming my skin again. Inflamed dermis is fully exposed, my penis throbbing. I can feel the ornamentation of the blood god, that was on my jacket, becoming a searing tattoo on my bare back. My seagull necklace is all that I am wearing.

My canine teeth are erect. I take the woman on the slab first. My lips find the pulse in her neck, the metal smell is so close now. Teeth part skin as the thick salty warm liquid flows everywhere. The blood tastes as it smells, only richer, warmed iron, each ferrous swallow enlarges my penis and hardens my muscles. My biceps and shoulders swell and I am getting stronger. I grasp her tightly as I drink. My whole body is pounding as she fades away.

The other is still at my back. Her clothes have evaporated too. Our bodies lock and are slippery with sweat. She maintains her embrace as I rise and turn to face her, immersed in lust, pressing my nose against her nape I take her scent first, teeth then separate skin. The warm salty liquid spills and spurts. Rubbing against her as I drink I think of Drew. My teeth go deeper. Our bodies merge. Hearts beat in synchronicity, as I drink I become harder and harder until there is an explosion of ecstasy that resonates through us both. My breath gushes from my nostrils as I do not want to stop the drink to breathe.

Our hearts lose each other, they were like two galloping horses running together. My heart remains beating fast as her slows. Moans of pleasure escape her lips, as the weight of her body in my arms becomes flaccid. Breathless, I let her fall.

Sweat becomes solid and I am clothed as before. The blood is still warm on my lips, my thoughts are rapid and clear, my movements are effortless and swift. I wipe my mouth on the sleeve of my jacket. The blood seeps into the leather. Rejuvenated, finding Drew is my only goal. Before leaving the room, I enter the bathroom one last time to look into the mirror. I expose

my teeth and flick one of my canines with my nail. I look into

my eyes again, *"Yep, must be in fucking Heaven."*

Life's residuum returned, white surgical room gone, the room

looks in death as it did in life. The cluttered futon is returned

along with the broken plaster walls. I see the door to the hallway

is ajar. I step through. Not much different here either. Hall with

several doors to other units. Wall sconce to my right with a bro-

ken light bulb. Stairs leading down to the entry hall in front of

me.

I wonder, were the events that just happened a dream? I feel

my teeth. Canines retracted. Claws are fingernails again. I'm

still clad in a dark leather jacket and boots. I feel my neck, find-

ing the charm. I closely examine it while I think about Drew.

The thought of him crushes my chest. In my mind I feel his lips

on mine while our bodies press tightly, removing all separation.

I set out down the dim stairway to the front hall. I pass the

empty mail boxes and make my exit.

The world hasn't changed that much at all. The sky is over-cast. You can look directly at the sun. A large silvery disk float-ing in the atmosphere, nearby clouds alight as if giving birth to an ovum. It could be the moon, but the presence of daylight lets me know this isn't so. Birds, squirrels, and people are going about their monotonous dance. *Are they dead too?*

My car is parked in the street. I put a hand into my jacket pocket and yank out keys. *"That's convenient."* I spurt out.

Bardo Boy

Drew! Drew!

Where are you? I had the worst dream last night.

You told me you didn't want to be with me anymore.

Days and nights of unreturned phone calls and letters.

I never felt so much pain from nothing, from no words,

no smells, no touch, no smiles...

I am trying to fix an old shirt,

one that I wore everyday so long ago.

I'm sewing it with beautiful threads of light,

warm smiles, a past, a future,

but the seams keep opening and

the buttons fall off,

I don't understand...

I am sooooo glad it was only a dream,

a remnant of insecurity that doesn't need repair.

It does however remind me of how much I love you,

and all the connections of yesterday and tomorrow

we share.

Book

Where does one start to look for a dead alcoholic? A bar. I jump into my Charger, torn leather bucket seats, a dusty dash board, and a broken cigarette lighter. I turn the key and rev the engine. The radio blasts, while the tires squeal as I pull away and head to Drew's favorite hang-out, Rose's.

Rose's is a neighborhood pub that caters to the locals, it's in walking distance for most of the patrons. Drew lived right around the corner. Outside, above the door, hangs a large translucent back lit sign with a single large black rose. "Rose's," is scribed in red, it weaves through the leaves and thorns of the large black rose.

Inside, it is always night, dark and cool. There is a persistent smell of stale beer and damp cardboard. Stacks of empty beer cases line the back walls, they look like a Philadelphia skyline after an evening of drinking. Actually, the whole place takes on new life after several beers and a couple of shots. Sloppy smiles, laughter, and conversations take on deeper meaning than if they occurred in sobering daylight.

The maroon and white checkered floor is often sticky. Tutor style shutters, made of amber plexiglas and brown plastic, cover the windows. An open staircase lines each of the side walls, they lead up to a second floor open loft that overlooks the bar. This is where Rose conducts her business. She sits at a dusty, cigarette coated, large desk that partially screens her from the events of the drinkers below.

Although there is daylight, the streetlights are shinning. I guess it is because of the overcast sky. While cruising, the overhead lights go out one by one as I approach them, at the same time my Charger feels drained of power and slows. My gas gauge shows half a tank. I barely make it to the side of the road as my engine dies. Frustrated, I try to restart my engine. *Dead, completely dead.* Grabbing my keys I open the door. I pop the hood from under the dashboard and put on my headlights to see if the battery has juice.

Making my way to the engine, the street is very quiet. Like a

Sunday morning in Upper Manhattan, no other cars or people.

Silence, just the motionless atmosphere and me. I thrust open

the hood, nothing looks wrong. The distributor cap is fine, the

spark plug wires are all attached firmly. But, the headlights are

out. *Drained battery?*

While inspecting the cables I hear giggling. looking up I see

that I have come to stop in front of a small storefront. "Printing

Press" is written on the window in gold lettering. The giggling is

coming from inside. I close my hood and listen closer.

There is a strange laughter. It sounds like a recorded child's

chuckling playing over and over, nervous and silly. I walk up

and find the door is unlocked and enter. The inside is completely

bare, it looks like its been abandoned for years. Gray linoleum

office tile floor, baseboard heating, several scattered papers lying

about the bare floor. There are stairs to the left of the entrance.

Climbing the stairs I follow the laughter, it suddenly stops and

the sound is replaced with the smell of smoke from a cigarette. I

reach the top and see a handsome man seated at a desk staring at me. He looks all business, suit, greased back blond hair. He is

sporting a salesman's smile.

"I was waiting for you." He says to me with his heavy

German accent.

His blue eyes look familiar. I find myself locked, looking into

his eyes, but I don't remember him.

Startled, I ask, *" Do I know you? "*

"Yes, and... No." His reply.

Smiling, he takes a deep drag from his filterless cigarette. I

watch the smoke escape his body, uncurling from his nose, a

horizontal plume exits from his mouth. He seems to be intensely

enjoying this moment, almost as if he can't contain himself. I

keep my distance. I don't trust him, but he's holding my atten-

tion.

He continues, *"You are looking for Drew? I want you to find*

Drew. I am here to help you. Your guide, so to speak." His

smile is unbroken as he takes another drag from his cigarette.

How does he know me and about my search for Drew? I relax,

trying to conceal my unease.

"I didn't know angels smoke." I say to him, probing.

"Who said I was an angel?...Bardo Boy." His smile is widening.

My discomfort is no longer concealed. I want answers. My

posture tightens. The smell of his cigarette is pissing me off.

My emotions are breaking free, anger and frustration rise, and

yet I am strangely...horny. I can feel every molecule in this

room, but I can't detect his smell or any sound coming from his

body. No blood in his veins. No heartbeat in his chest. Just

fucking cigarette smoke. I study him closely trying to get a

grasp of who he is, while my skin burns and my heart races...

"Bardo Boy...? My Guide...? How do you know I'm looking

for Drew?" I ask, my voice deepening.

"Calm yourself Bardo Boy. We became comrades a long time ago. You need me, without me you are a formless vapor. Trust me." His incessant smiling continues.

He takes another drag. The smoke sputters from his lips. I watch the blue hue of the gas dance in the air. Thick clouds become thin wisps before fading away into nothingness.

He continues, *"I was there at the moment you were conceived, up until your death. After your death we became temporarily separated, but I found you. I was the one who woke you from that dark sleep. You are my protege. Wherever you go, I am there. Whatever you see, I see..."* He pauses, sitting forward in the chair, *"As for the name Bardo Boy... let's just say it is a personal indulgence... don't you like the name?"* His smile turns to laughter.

Looking at the charm around my neck, he stamps out his cigarette and rises from the chair. His eyes move to meet my eyes. His smile softening, a little more serious. His stare is arousing, it makes my mind lazy. A small draft moves past me.

Through my daze I realize he is behind me. I feel a firmness ex-

erting itself against my back. His elbow comes around my neck.

His other arm is reaching around my waist, squeezing me before

working its way to my groin. His movement to me was swift

and effortless. My anger melts as I enjoy his touch.

His whispers are at my neck, his breath caressing me... *"I will*

call you Bardo Boy... and you can call me... Book."

An electric tingle jumps from his lips and enters my skin re-

laxing me more.

"Book." I repeat.

His one hand has a soft grip on my crotch, his lips are at the

chain around my neck. *"The chain..."* He says.

Holding the back of his hand, I push it harder into my awak-

ening erection. *"What about it?"* I ask.

He clasps my groin firmly in his hand and commands, *"Take it off."*

Without hesitation I release my hold on his hand working my erection. Reaching up to remove the chain is when the clamoring begins.

First barely present, like a blowing car horn waking a sleeper. It starts out in the distance, not unlike a dream, before becoming louder into full blown consciousness.

Book breaks his grip on me, backing off, holding his head. The sound is no longer a horn, more like a gong. Repetitious. A beat, followed by a reverberation, then another beat. This has Book distressed. He is backing away with a painful look. He mentions something about an old man before fading into the wall behind him. His eyes lock onto mine before completely disappearing.

What the fuck? How I could have let myself become so vulnerable? I grasp the chain in my fist for good luck. I race down the stairs and outside to resume my search for Drew. It's dark. I wonder how long I was in the office. The street lights are back on, as well as my car's headlights. I climb into my Charger and turn the key. It starts up without a problem. I peel away with a screech and head to Rose's.

I'm a block away and I can hear the music blaring from the bar. *Looks like a good crowd tonight.* I park across the street and head for the door. Same old sign, "Rose's." There is a large door man. He must be about six foot ten and broad. His tee-shirt is two sizes too small. His bristly back hair curls up through his collar. *Is that fur?* It's as if he hears my thoughts. He turns around to face me. Large grooves course his face like sand dunes in the desert, huge pig like nose, several of his bottom teeth jut out pass his upper lip. "Bitch" is written across the front of his shirt. *Same old crowd.*

"Sorry buddy... Private party." He says, as he raises his arm to block my entrance. I whiz past him. My speed catches him by surprise and he's irritated. Two of his friends, equally as pretty, are at my sides. I know I can take them, but I figure it's easier to talk.

"I'm here to see Rose." I try to explain.

The three look at each other and laugh. *"Rose ain't in at the moment,"* he says, as the two grab me and usher me towards the door.

"You really are a bitch." I say to the fury pig face one.

Now I am the one who's irritated. I wrap my arms around the two and lock their elbows, this stops their advance. My rage expands through my skin, it makes the Heruka emblem on my jacket glow bright red, with teeth erect, breath steaming, and back straight, I come down on one knee snapping their arms. They wail out. The patrons, aware of the scuffle, back away and take it all in as if it's an extreme fighting match without the cage.

One of the customers sees my glowing emblem and yells out, *"He is a Blood Drinker. He has Heruka on his back."* I release the two and advance for the big bitch. His attitude changes and is humble now. He backs away with a bowing gesture, his arm submissively waving as he says, *"I didn't know you was with He-*

ruka... Please come in."

A little more calm, the emblem fades back to a leather carv-

ing, but my teeth remain erect. My guard is up as I make my

way through the crowd. The spectacle is over and the patrons

resume their partying. Although, my senses are at their peek, the

crowd on the other hand seems to be subdued. They are intoxi-

cated, in-between sleep and wake. There is a red sedating mist

that wafts in the barroom air.

Heading to the bar I pass through an ocean of corpses. Not

rotting, more like an experiment on the human design. There

may be an extra ear or an ear placed "in a new and improved po-

sition." Eyes encircling a head like a floral pagan crown. A

pretty woman with a tiny mouth, tiny until she smiles, then her

grin enlarges to take up most of her face.

There is a crippled, feeble, young man in a wheelchair. He is

twenty something, but looks to be ten years old, thin and flop-

ping over to one side in the chair. He looks to be sleeping in his

chair, not stirred by all the jostling going on around him. I can tell he houses a soul that runs deeper than his frail body looks to hold. Seeing him reminds me of Paul after the accident. I wonder If my mother and Paul are here, though I don't sense them. *Will I ever see them again?*

When I get to the bar the jukebox music stops and is replaced with scuffling feet, throats clearing, and glasses clinking. Numerous conversations merge and sound like a low pitch mumble. Through the noise a guitar plays.

The song grabs everyone by surprise. The vibrations, beautiful and warm, spread out affecting all that can hear it. Scuffling stops, the roar of mumbling fades and is replaced with a soothing string melody, followed by a guttural moaning. A large circle forms in the bar around the guitar player. I'm also moved by the music and want to see who is playing. Cutting back through the crowd I see smiles and heads nodding yes to each other; they all agree that it's talent that they're observing.

I pierce the line and see the boy that was in the wheelchair, standing naked. He is about four foot tall. He sways in the center of the crowd with his guitar that matches him in size. His legs have been amputated just above the knees. They have light brown leather straps running down the sides of his thighs that end in dull metal caps covering his stubs. His eyes are closed and shallow, as if he is blind. He shifts his weight from stump to stump as his sings. His body contorts into martyr like positions while moans escape his lips, it's as if he sacrificing his physical structure for the music.

Someone in the audience accompanies him with a tambourine, in doing so the entire bar falls deeper into the musical spell. The crowd gathers around the show clearing a path to the barkeep. The music is alluring, but I break from its influence. I have to stay focused on my search for Drew. I make my way to the barkeep, hoping that he has seen Drew.

The barkeep looks nice enough, human. He is a large man in his late thirties, not as big as the front door bitch, but tall and very solid. He has an Irish look about him. Rusted red hair. Strong forearms. Green eyes. He has his elbows on the bar, bent forward watching the crowd fall under the singer's charm. He straightens his stance as I approach and asks me, *"What can I get you?"*

"Some show." I reply

"Yea, Paul is always a crowd pleaser. That's, when he de-cides to sing."

Paul?

The barkeep continues, *"He doesn't talk much. Mostly hangs around in the wheelchair sleeping. That lady over there is the one who brings him here."*

I look over at the woman the barkeep is referring too. It is the woman with the expanding mouth that I saw earlier.

"I don't know him personally. Some of the regulars said his name was Paul."

I think about my brother Paul and his wheelchair. It's too much of a coincidence, but they look nothing like my mother and Paul. I don't have the same sense that they are here as I do for Drew. I leave that thought and return to my search for Drew.

"I'm looking for somebody. He died a long time ago."

"Jumping fucking Jesus buddy! Did ya try the cemetery?"

His response surprises and frustrates me. I try to work it out in my head... I know I'm dead and I'm talking to this guy... so, he must be dead too. If I am to spend an eternity *here* I want to spend it with Drew. This bartender may be able to help me find him. I am so close. My skin simmers. My heart is beating wildly... if this asshole...! I take a deep breath and get my composure back. Changing my inquiry a bit, with an added fake chuckle, I continue.

"What I mean to say is... he hung out here a long time ago...."

The bartender, with a suspicious expression on his face, turns
his back to me and places a bottle on the shelf as he replies, *"I
said, try the fucking cemetery."*

Looking at his broad back, ignoring me, brings on that gnawing that I experienced in my bathroom. Without thought, I reach
over the bar and grasp him by the back of his shoulder. He slips
rearwards though the air. I bend him over the bar exposing his
neck. His head lay across the bar's rail.

Frightened, he struggles to get free. He tries to rise, but I
hold him in place with one arm. His chest is firm and wide. I
can make out his tight form through his Rose's tee-shirt, it feels
hard under my hand. I open his neck with my bite. Warm ecstasy fills me. It hasn't been that long since my last feeding, but
I already forgot the beauty of this sensation. It all comes back
with a sanquineous rush.

I can smell and taste the metals that are mixed with the beer
in his blood, with the first drop the euphoric moments with two
women in my apartment returns to me. My dick engorges. The

first droplets are immediately replaced with a spurting gush that completely fills my mouth after each swallow, as I drink he relaxes and submits. I run my hand from his chest to his groin and feel his equally hard erection. His moans are soaked with pleasure. I dig into him deeper, he moans louder.

"*Oh god...Oh god,*" escapes his lips.

His groin is wet with cum. I feel the warmness soaking through the fabric. The boy's music fills everyones mind, while the bartender's scent of blood and cum fills the air. His groans are his own song. Squeezing his crotch harder brings me closer to my own crest. Loud horns blow. The sound is monotonous and crude, like an ancient Roman revelry going to war.

In the first few moments I believe the horns are part of the boy's ballad, then I realize they are not. Ecstasy is replaced with stillness. Stillness is replaced by dullness.

I am standing in the bar holding air as the horns continue. The bar is empty except for me and the horns. The Irish barkeep gone, crippled boy gone, even the big bitch is gone. No evidence of any recent event is present. In fact, Rose's looks to have been vacant for years. Cold, dank and dusty like an old western saloon in a ghost town.

My neck is weighed down, as my seagull charm pulses an incandescent blue. The pulsations follow the crescendo-decrescendo of the horns. The light from the pendant grows brighter while Rose's becomes harder to see. The pendent's illumination darkens the bar and opens a new setting. Maroon and white tile floor is replaced with carpet. Walls appear where there were none. The horns blare louder and louder. I see an old asian man. He looks to be meditating. He looks like an old friend of my dad.

Water begins to fill the bar, rising quickly. The exit door and windows are gone. Blackness now replaces carpet and walls as the water swirls around my knees. My breath is rapid and is being pulled from my lungs. I struggle to hold the air in my chest in between gasps. A foul odor boils from the water, it makes me retch all the blood I had just taken. While gulping for air I take in the smell of cigarettes. I look up and see Book. He is floating

in the blackness. For better or worse the sight of him relieves

my discomfort.

"Bardo Boy, listen to me. Get rid of the chain."

An inner voice tells me this is wrong, but I know the alterna-

tive can't be good. Death in a cesspool again. Perhaps, real

death this time. Oblivion. I'm slipping away. I don't know

where I am, but I know Drew is *here* and I am so close to finding

him. I know this water will take me away from Drew, so I grab

the chain. Book's grin grows. I look down into the water. The

smell is awful. My decision is made. Just as I rip the charm

from my neck I glimpse the crippled singer and woman in my

peripheral vision, they look like Paul and my mother. Too late,

the necklace is off and flying into the darkness.

The bar is returned to as it was. The audience is still held

captive by the music. A drained Irish barkeep lies across the bar.

My tongue is removing the last of the blood from my lips. I feel

a hand from behind as it comes to rest on my shoulder. I turn to
see Book smiling. I return the smile.

"Let's go find your boyfriend, Drew," he says to me. We
weave our way through the bar and exit into the night filled
street. *"We make a pretty good team, you and me,"* he continues,
while pulling me close.

He offers me one of his self rolled cigarettes. I hesitate. I
never did like tobacco smoke, but hell... I never liked blood either. I put the cigarette in between my lips as Book produces the
fire. I take a drag and inhale deeply, hold it for a moment before
letting it exit my body. A sense of invincibility courses through
my veins. The pungent aroma of the smoke mixes with the taste
of the bartender's blood in my mouth like a good wine with a
hearty meal. My dick, still full, pushes against my pants as we
walk. After all, I never did get to cum. I turned to Book and
calmly demand, *"Take me to Drew."*

Hell

INTER-BARDO LOG #2

Well, it looks like I have Bardo Boy under wraps. I know I said I was in full control earlier, but occasionally I do run into obstacles. The old man is giving me more problems than I expected. He has broken from his prison. Perhaps your reading is affecting the others as much as it affects me. You might be making them more solid than I thought could be possible. No problem, as I said Bardo Boy and I are forever intertwined. This is for the best. I couldn't let him drown in his own dirty sewage, now could I? Hum?

You wonder, why do I want the charm gone? Why was the old man trying to drown him? I can't tell you these things. You might tell Bardo Boy. Oh, I know you wouldn't tell him on purpose. But, your minds are linked. Even though he is unaware of your world, you may still affect him subconsciously. Best to keep you in the dark. Bardo Boy is mine.

END INTER-BARDO LOG #2

Book and I walk together for what feels like miles. Exploring the land, I look upon houses, humans, beasts, human-beasts...

"What is this place?" I ask Book.

"It's all you Bardo Boy. It is all created in your image. You are the ruling God here. It is your world, a place to take any and all pleasures that come your way. Call it what you like."

"I'm the boss?"

"You are the boss."

"Then bring Drew here."

"It's not that easy."

"I thought you said I was the boss?"

"Even the boss has rules to follow. The Universe houses God. It's not the other way around. When in someone's house you must follow the house rules. For example, you can bleed or fuck anybody you like. This world, your world, will accommodate your needs. Resurrecting the dead is another story, but rules can be broken... with a little help from a friend," Book says with a wide grin.

"Where are we going then?"

"Where do you want to go?"

"Home, I just want to go home... I'm tired."

"OK. Stand still with your eyes closed. Now click your heels together three times and say there's no place like ho..."

I flash Book a sarcastic grin and shove him playfully.

"This isn't fucking OZ, Book!"

That said. My jacket tears as muscles bulge, fingers become claws, and arms rip from their sleeves. The jacket is pulled behind me as skin ignites. Naked from the waist up, black biker jacket transforms into black leathery wings. The Heruka emblem burns from my back through to my chest and glows blood-red. I ascend into the sky so quickly, it feels like I have left my body behind. It takes me a moment to realize that I am airborne. Book is standing where I left him. I survey the sky. When I look back, Book is gone.

I am revived as I swim through the dense clouds. My face explodes with tiny bursts of sensations. It reminds me of walking out on a rainy day just after shaving off a beard.

I soar up and watch as the earth grows smaller and the clouds thin. I turn my gaze upwards. There is a gibbous moon, blue-white and bright. There is a thick band of stars sprayed across the sky. Looking down again, the moon light reflects off the quilted surface of the billowy cloud masses. The reflection creates an atmosphere of silvery blue radiance.

I want to stay here forever and mingle with the elements. My mind is resting somewhere outside my body. Moments before, I wanted to go home, but home could never feel like this. I am untethered from time. All reference points lost.

I remember when I was alive, dozing off in a dark room before a shift at work and the confusion after jerking awake thinking I missed my shift. Looking at the alarm clock while still in a daze I wouldn't know if it was seven in the morning or seven at night. The peacefulness that follows when the mind clears, and I know I am not late, and I can continue my slumber, this is where I am. A mindless sojourn. I'm staring into the clouds, they begin to have a purposeful movement. A scene from my life when I was with Drew is being played.

We were in high school. My life was pretty shitty. Paul and my mom were gone. My dad was always working. I wasn't the smartest kid in the school. I wasn't good at sports and definitely wasn't the coolest. I was a nerd. Isolation, that's the best way to describe it. I was set apart from my family by death and my

dad's work. I was set apart from my peers, by... though I didn't

fully know it at the time, my sexuality. Years later new friends

were always surprised that I was gay, but in high school the kids

always seemed to know, even before I did. I was set apart from

from the entire human race. Until I met Drew.

It was the first day of high school during locker assignments

when I saw Drew. I wanted to know him more, though I didn't

understand why at the time. It was like an impulse or an instinct.

I wonder if it was because he looked like one of the cool kids,

but was sitting alone like me, or maybe it was destiny.

The rule was two students to a locker. The entire class was

partnered up leaving four students unpaired. Two boys and two

girls, as in gym class I was always left unchosen. The girls were

Marcia and Patty. Marcia was a compulsive hair chewer and shy.

Patty had braces, thick glasses, blonde stringy hair, body odor,

and an aggressive temper. She had once given a kid a concus-

sion when she pushed him backwards over his chair. She was a nazi nerd. Next to them stood Drew and me. I couldn't believe my luck. It was Drew and me sharing a locker for an entire year.

Everything came to a halt, I was awakened from my fantasy when I heard the teacher say, *"Great. Four of you... Let's mix it up. Drew is with Marcia. Patty with..."*

It was life fucking with me again. Patty made it immediately known at the lockers that she gets the lower shelf. It wasn't a school, it was a prison and I was Patty's bitch. The good news was that she stood at least a foot shorter than me. I knew I could take her down in self-defense if I had too.

Drew and Marcia's locker was next to Patty's and mine. While I waited my turn to access the locker, Patty wrestled with her books, my gaze turned towards Drew. Our eyes met first. His face was so beautiful. Next, our ears met as we acknowledged each other with a nervous hello. I will never forget those first few moments. Drew spoke with pursed lips trying to hide his braces. The cover of his note book was wet with hand prints from his nervous sweat.

Drew and I shared a place in that timeline, both of us existed on the edge of an alternate reality that was high school. Everyone else seemed to thrive, where Drew and I merely survived.

We became great friends and eventually lovers. Life was great on that edge with Drew. We shared many good years until his death. The last several years were a bit shaky because of his drinking, but I loved him anyway. I would find myself during the quiet parts of my days just thinking about him. *I have to find him.*

I descend. Wind rips across me ventrally as clouds rise swiftly. The air spills around my face while small gushes enter my nostrils and fill my lungs, it's almost as refreshing as a swallow of blood.

A moment passes and I'm not moving. Air and clouds are rushing by me, but I can't see the ground. It's as if I am still and everything else is moving. I pull in my wings in an attempt to dive. *Am I just at a higher altitude?* My actions seem to have an opposite effect. The faster I travel the more lost I become. The clouds thin into a blackness. I'm surrounded in darkness. There are no stars or moonlight to guide me. While I drift Book speaks

to me, *"Bardo Boy. I am taking you to Drew."*

"I thought resurrection was difficult?" I remind Book of his
earlier words.

"To be with Drew you must leave your world to enter his.

This is not without great risk. You can become permanently lost.

Drew ...let's say, wasn't in the best state of mind at the time of his

death."

"And I was?"

"No, but you had my help. Drew is alone. He is different,

changed from what you remember."

"...As long as there aren't any bars we will be fine."

"This isn't a joke Bardo Boy, his world is fucked up. A pure

hell realm. You will be vulnerable. He is the God in his self in-

duced reality. You will be nothing more than a pawn. He may

not have any memory of who he was while he was alive."

I tumble as the clouds return. Projections of my life and

death play over and over. I see images of an old Asian man. The

same man I saw in the bar, when I tossed my necklace. This vi-

sion is different from the memory clouds. This image seems to

be real, not just a vision from the past. The old man's lips are

moving, but I can't make out what he is saying. *Evan?*

I am falling faster, spinning, streaking like a meteor. The old

Asian man keeps pace, but is fading away. I hit the ground hard.

The earth is firm, but gives way softening my impact. A perfect

landing. I am crouched to the ground on bent knee and finger

tips. Like a knight kneeling before his king. Dust rises around

me. Wings revert to black biker jacket.

I see before me on the ground a shimmering piece of metal.

The dust falls, as it settles it dulls the glint of the metal that is half buried in the ground. I brush away the dirt and discover a chain. I pull it from its resting place. It's my seagull. I don't understand why it should be here, but I instinctively know not to let Book know about this. Besides, I'm in Drew's world now. I shouldn't need Book anymore. Standing up I place the charm around my neck. It comes to rest against my chest and burns my skin. I let out a howl as it melts, it seeps under my dermis.

The day is bright and clear. The sun feels good as it grazes my skin. I'm standing on a hill along a dirt road. Green fields, dark and lush roll on down to a forest about a mile away. I study the tree line and the meadow before it. I have never seen grass this green. I take it all in; the white clouds drift slowly. I follow their shadows as they move across the glowing green hill. The shadows partially darken the hill as they float. The sky is blue. A blue that permeates and surrounds everything.

"Some fucked up world. ...looks like someone has been to an AA meeting or two."

Leaving the road I encounter a little girl sitting in the grass with a daisy. Her blonde curly hair frames her porcelain skin. She is in an eighteenth century dress that is bordered with ribbons. She looks up to me and smiles as I draw near to her. Her eyes are as blue as this day's sky. She offers me the flower she is holding.

Nice day to drink blood... I think to myself as I return her smile.

Standing over her I bend to one knee and accept her gift of petals. She is unmoved and continues to smile. She is making it easy. So quiet though, I do not hear her heartbeat. My senses liven. My chest heaves. The scent of earth and chlorophyl mingle. The thought of blood is the forefront of my attention.

Just as I lean into her I feel a large impact to my right side. The horizon turns vertically. I am down. A large hairy weight has me pinned to the ground. Its hot breath smells like it has eaten something that died a thousand times. I look up as it licks my face, *"Derry? Derry! Fucking Christ!"* Droplets explode

from my eyes as I grab this hairy beast. I haven't seen Derry

since the day he was killed and Paul was maimed. Sobbing, I

hold Derry tight pushing my face into his side. I am afraid that

this is a dream and I'll wake up holding air. He lets out a bark. I

open my eyes. Paul and my mom stand beside me.

Paul is healed, just as he was before the accident. My mom is

in the dress she was buried in. Her face is radiant. We embrace

while tears flow. The little girl runs away giggling. I think I

recognize the laughter, it is melodic and unnatural, but Paul and

Mom hold my attention.

I kiss the top of Paul's head. I breath in his aroma while his

hair sticks to my tear soaked face. Derry is barking and jumping

in circles. Paul leaves my grip to return Derry's affection. My

arms are around Mom.

My grip tightens, as I can't get enough of her, it has been so

long since I saw her. I look deeply into her face. Her expression

turns from joy to fear as she tries to push me away. I bury my

face into the hollow of her neck and breathe deeply. I become

lost in her scent, so much that I do not notice her struggling. I do
not notice Paul pounding and pulling on my back or Derry's incessant barking.

I feel a deep ache that makes me release my grip, followed by
the awareness of my mother's knee in my groin. I howl as I
strike out with the back of my hand. This sends my mom back-
ward in flight, followed by a spray of her blood. I step forward
and pick her up, without thought I hit her again, like a game of
kick the can.

The smell of blood has me fully erect. Derry is biting at my
back. I turn and hit him once, shredding his coat along his side,
he releases a whimper. Paul runs to Derry's aid and falls to the
ground wailing as he lies across Derry's limp body.

Mom is on hands and knees, slowly crawling away. I follow,
walking behind. Her dress is tattered and trails after her. I step
on it. It falls off like a snake shedding its skin. Grabbing her
with handful of hair, I mount her. She wails as I enter her from
behind. I feel a blood rush with each thrust, it makes my neck

throb and my head explode with ecstasy. My teeth bury themselves everywhere my lips can reach and I drink.

Finished and breathless, I collapse against the motionless
lump under me. My heart is still beating fast. I rise on all fours
and see my mother lying below me. Her blood covering me as if
I was just born. Like a title wave rushing back to shore, the rec-
ognition of what I have just done floods my head. I am drown-
ing in my realization.

"What the fuck?"

I collapse against my mother again, this time in grief, scream-
ing my apologies over and over. The look of horror on her face
and the betrayal in her eyes, as I crushed her throat, replays in
my mind. I rise up onto my knees and look to the sky through a
veil of tears. The sky is still a perfect blue. Soft white clouds
meander slowly... peacefully.

I turn to look back. Paul is standing behind Derry's limp
body. He is bawling. He has the same look in his eyes as my

mom's did, but with equal amounts of anger added. I can tell he

is trying to banish me with his stare. I rise and reach out to him,

but before I can call his name he runs off towards the woods.

Book warned me about this, *"fucked up,"* world. I should have

been more aware, more alert.

"BOOK! Book where the fuck are you?"

"I am here. I am always here Bardo Boy."

I turn to see Book looking at the woman and beast carnage.

He looks back at me.

"Don't look so sad, you've got what you wanted, what you

asked for. You are in his world... let us find Drew together."

Book says trying to comfort me.

"Drew? I don't give a fuck about Drew right now. Is this shit

real? Is that my mother?" I scream at Book.

"It would appear so. It is unfortunate that our sobering experiences are acts that hurt ourselves and the ones we love. The place where this comprehension occurs... is true Hell. You were warned."

I fall to my knees next to my mother's body.

"Come, come with me..." Books says as he tries to get me to leave my mothers side. *"Let's find Drew. He went running towards the woods."*

"That was Drew? The little girl?"

Pictures and words enter my head and leave as new words and pictures arrive. My focus has been obliterated. Nothing makes sense.

"Drew set this up?"

"I told you he was changed and dangerous."

My legs have become dull weights. I am unable to move my limbs or my mind past this moment. My breathing is rapid. I hold my head while narrowing thoughts bombard my skull. *Blood, throbbing penis, mother, revulsion, love, sweat, brother, shit, breath, regret, loss...*

"Bardo Boy," Book shouts.

The sound barely makes it through the static of the musings invading my brain. *What kind of sick fuck has Drew become? How can he make me do anything as horrible as this?*

I try to convince myself that somewhere inside him there is a piece of us that remains, but my head is boiling and my body is burning. A whirlwind is rising. It tears open my jacket and sends it flapping to my back. My chest expands as my arms and legs bulge. Claws emerge from my fingers. Teeth become erect,

I know they glisten in this light of this perfect day. Bardo Boy is

fully formed...

"Drew, if you can hear me, I coming for you."

The Forest

I launch from the ground, tearing through atmosphere, and head towards the forest. To the place where Book saw Drew, as the little girl, running. Mental pictures of me opening Drew, drinking him, spilling him are filling my head. I rein in my thoughts and focus on my task of finding him. I reach the front line of trees and pass them like a fighter jet in an air show.

I turn my gaze away from the forest to look directly into the sun, challenging it. A self destructive move, an attempt to burn out the images of my mother dying by my hands. The light is blinding me with its painful brilliance, but I keep them open. My tears run as if trying to put out a fire.

When the brightness dims and the contrast returns, I'm surprised to find myself standing in a room with the old Asian man. He is fondling the seagull charm around my neck, its glint is the last of the remaining radiance. I'm human again.

"I see you have found your necklace." He says to me smiling.

"Who are you and where am I?"

"These are questions everyone should ask themselves... To answer your first question, I am a friend of your father's. The second question is more difficult to explain."

"Evan... I remember you now."

He lets the charm fall back around my neck while memories climb their way to the forefront of my mind. My thoughts are tranquil and soothing. He was in business with my dad, but left to pursue a spiritual life. I never took the time to know him myself. I was always off in my own space of delusional self pity or totally devoting my time to Drew. I blamed my dad and his work for our separation. Now I know I was at fault too. My death must have really fucked him up.

I snap back from my memories. *Is this another Drew trick?* First he makes me beat and sodomize my mother, and now this. Who wants to be the first to ride the guilt-a-whirl? I'm waiting for my dad to step in so I can beat and fuck him to death too.

This is indeed a fucked up world. Nonetheless, if he really is my

dad's friend or just another trick, he may help me find Drew.

"Why is this charm so interesting to you?" I ask.

*"The charm may represent your true nature, your true self. It
could be a clue to future or past connections that are important
for entering the Bliss State, your way out of the bardos. That is
for you to discover. "*

"Bardos? Book calls me Bardo Boy."

*"The bardos are your prison, my prison. Any being that is
conscious is subject to the bardos. The bardos are the hardest
prisons to escape, because you do not even know you are being
held. Book? Is this what he calls himself? He is your prison
keeper, your Great Faker. No doubt he has kept you from entering the Bliss State."*

"Prison? What have I done?"

Laughing he replies, *"Your crimes are that you are a human that hasn't found peace, just like most others. I am doing all I can to help break you out. I have been doing the practice of One with the Heruka gong trying to shatter your illusions..."*

The expression on the old man's face turns from jovial to frustration, as the floor explodes into a kaleidoscope of wooden splinters. A pine odor fills the room.

Tree branches break through the floor and entwine my legs and waist. The large tendrils tear my pants and skin as they wind around me, like shark skin, tasting their meal as they encircle it.

Rage mounts as I am squeezed. The first violent tug downward pulls my bottom half through the floor. I struggle like a mouse in the grip of a snake. I resist while transforming into Bardo Boy. The seagull charm retreats under my skin. My wings are now fully extended, lapping at the air, trying to gain ground. Each snare I am able to break is replaced with three as I am ripped through the floor.

The old man and room are gone. I am airborne, over the forest in the grip of the trees. Their cable-like branches reaching far up over the forest canopy. My wings beat uselessly as I am dragged down. My decent through the top of the trees brings more tentacles. The more I resist the tighter the grip. I am pulled under the forest canopy while filtered light shimmers all around me. Leaves rip from their appendages and drop like green snowflakes. My journey comes to an end as I am secured against the base of an old tree, its deep furrowed skin pressing into my back, wings pinned to my sides.

Sitting before me, reticent, on a large square stone is the little girl. Her lap is full of plucked petals. The green leafy snowflakes continue their downward drift. The stippled light coming from above highlights her blond curls in transient bursts of yellow, as the disembodied leaves settle quietly around her. She is focused on the flower in her hand.

It's as if I am not here. She plucks one petal from the flower's center, examines it before letting it fall to the others in her lap. She moves to the next, repeating the act. My body is throbbing with pain. Each exhalation releases a crack as my ribs break.

"Drew." I call to her, but no response. She is immersed in the flower. *"Drew..."* *Is he fucking deaf?*

I struggle against the tree. The pain is unbearable. I expand my chest and wings stretching the tendrils, but they snap me back. I let out a roar of pain. The little girl pauses her mechanical task and looks up at me blankly. The blond curls sparkle as rays of sunlight come and go about her head. She crushes the flower in her tiny hand. Her mouth opens under a stony stare and lets out a demented chattering.

"Drew... What the fuck! Why are you doing this?"

She rises from her slab. Petals fall from her lap, dusting her shoes. She turns away, dropping the crumpled flower from her hand and skips into the forest. The tree releases its grip as she departs. I slide to the ground landing on hands and knees. I gather my strength to follow her, but she fades from sight before I can get up.

Her departure is replaced with a amorous scent. The phero-mone arouses me and relieves my pain. I look up to the slab. A beautiful naked man occupies the large stone. *A peace offering from Drew?* He is lying in repose, propped up on his elbows. His skin is devoid of all color. He is erect, his swelling pointing to his navel. A taught ball sack rests between his legs. His firm belly paves a way up to his broad chest. When I look into his face I see a playful grin. He is enjoying my visual pleasure. He lets out a laugh when our eyes meet. His teeth also erect, a Blood Drinker.

I follow the perfume to his armpit and bury my nose, inhaling deeply as I rub his sweat across my face. My wings retreat. He removes me from the hollow under his arm and moves his mouth to my hollow, then his lips trail to my chest. I feel his breath against my skin as he bites into my nipple. A warm trickle runs down my chest to my belly. I smell the blood as he suckles. He maintains his grip on my chest with his mouth and removes my jacket, letting it fall to the ground.

"Fucking Christ...he's drinking me." The sharp pains from my nipple come rhythmically and travel to my throbbing penis. I grasp his head and pull him harder into my breast. His skin pinkens. He reaches down to my erection and takes a firm hold through my pants. I let out a gasp followed by a moan.

He opens my pants to expose my stiffening penis. The blood from my nipples runs down to my groin, lubricating his grip. He has hold of both our cocks. I bury my face into his neck. His warm blood fills my mouth, each swallow increases the sensitivity in my groin. I collapse against him with my full weight, drinking from his neck and fucking his blood filled hand. He lets out his cry as orgasms explode in my head and in his hand. Breathless, we collapse to our stoney bed still entwined. I fall unconscious.

I am in a room, it looks like a waiting area in a 1940's publishing office. Tacky plastic plants in several of the corners. Wall paper curling with a yellow sickness. Dirty windows. The overhead fluorescent lighting is being filtered by a nicotine tanned plastic cover. Large stained sofas face each other in the middle of the room, they are separated by a decaying wooden table littered with dying magazines. A row of rusted filing cabinets line one wall. There are no doors. The smell of ink permeates the air.

I suppose I am dreaming. It has been so long since I slept. Whoever it was that said, *"I'll have enough time to sleep when I'm six feet under,"* was dead wrong. When I think about it my life and death are dream like, a dream with varying levels of consciousness.

A large metallic floor fan occupies one of the corners, its pull chain taps at its wire cage keeping tempo with the hum of the spinning blades, as I listen to its drumming I realize I'm not alone. I can barely make it out at first, as the sound is softer than the hum. The sound is coming from the fan, a whisper mingling

with its turbulence. I move closer trying to hear the whisper better. It's getting louder, but I can't make out any sensible words.
Sounds more like... baby chatter... No, baby laughter. I pull the
chain to stop the fan and the laughter halts. I turn to find an exit
from this room.

I search the walls for an opening when the laugher returns, as
I try to find its source the laughter grows louder. It is deafening.
It's the little girl from the forest... Drew. The pain it induces is
not in my ears or in my head. It is not a physical pain, although
it makes me react physically trying to escape its influence.

It's an emotional pain. The heart stopping pain of finding
your love's suicide letter. A pain that tells you, *"this is it. It's
you and me babe, from here on out..."* You know the future is
changed forever. You want to go back, trying to rework past
scenarios in your head, *if I tried harder, or if I didn't kick him out
for the drinking,* as if it would have made a difference.

I wake up alone on the slab, tearful. The night has come. The
air around me cools my sweaty skin. I fasten my clothes and lay
on my back against my hard bed looking into the night sky.

The forest's lullaby is soothing, much better than the deranged

little girl's laughter that woke me from my nightmare. Some-

thing doesn't feel right though. The smell of ink and the laugher

from my dream along with my vision of Evan lingers in my

mind... *She isn't Drew.* I rise from the slab to find demented

Goldilocks.

Drew

I navigate the forest with ease. Moonlight illuminates my way. I head down the same path taken by the girl. The scent of the sun leaving the earth fills the night air, each species of tree releases its unique fragrance. Eyes, wings, legs, and tails go about their forest business. While trying to track the little girl, my mind is replaying scenes from my life. I'm with Drew on the day we graduated high school, in the gym auditorium just after the ceremony. Families still occupied the roll out bleachers while we escaped under them.

"Follow me." He said with a grin on his face. That smile always sucked me in. He grabbed me by my gown and pulled me into the men's locker room that was just around the corner. In the locker room, he spun me around and pressed his body against mine until I was pinned against the cold tile wall.

He reached under his gown and pulled out a bottle of blackberry brandy. He took a mouth full and passed me the bottle. I didn't care about drinking that much, Drew was my drink, but whatever made him happy made me happy. The blackberry brandy was overly sweet, as if the sugar was there to cover the taste of the cheap alcohol used to make it, which it didn't; it tasted like cough syrup. But, I drank because Drew drank.

"What do you want to do tomorrow now that we're free?" He asked, after taking another large swig.

"I don't know, I wasn't really thinking about tomorrow."

"Let's go down the shore." He offered.

"Sounds good to me." I said, and took my turn at a mouthful of brandy.

He looked into my eyes, It made me so horny. He had me in a full body embrace as we kissed. The bottle of brandy pressed into my back, pinned against me and the tile wall. But, I didn't care, because I was in his arms.

He took my upper lip between his teeth and grabbed me tighter. He held me in his arms and mouth as if we would never see each other again, as if it were our last moment together. Our breath merged, then our bodies. I felt him in my mind and I know he felt me in his.

Our embrace broke when the door to the locker room flew open. It was Patty, my old locker mate. Drew had stolen the blackberry brandy from Patty and she had come to retrieve it. When she saw us against the wall she screamed, *"Queers,"* then speed out into the gym to blast the news of what she had just seen. Drew grabbed me by my hand as we fled.

No one paid much attention to Patty. She didn't push it too much anyway, after all, she was in the men's locker room looking for a bottle of brandy she shouldn't have had.

The next day Drew and I drove to the shore, after convincing my dad to loan me his car, a reward for graduating. We spent the day laying in the sun watching the waves come and go. Drew loved listening to the seagulls. He heeded their calls, while I wrote poems.

Blood God

I'm tracking the little girl, when I pick up the scent of cigarettes. *Is Book here?* He said he is always here, that he hears
and sees everything I do. But, I'm not buying it. *The laughing.*
I heard that giggling the first time when I met Book at the Printing Press office when my car broke down. It was the laughter
that lured me inside. *It's Book.* It was fucking Book all along.
Evan told me he was my *"prison keeper."* There is noway Drew
is responsible for this world. How could I even for a moment
have believed it?

The path I'm following is more organized, a walkway that has
been worn into the forest floor. It leads to a clearing, as I walk I
rack my brain. *How can I put an end to Book?* He said that
without him I'm a *"formless vapor,"* that I need him. But, Book
is the obstacle between Drew and me.

I enter the clearing and see rows and rows of gray stone
markers. They are imbedded in the forest floor like tombstones.
All are hand chiseled with writing, symbols, and diagrams cover-

ing the entire surface of every stone. There must be hundreds of them. They make a pattern that would be more obvious if viewed from above, like the Nazca lines in Peru. Only, no monkey symbols here, spiders or birds. No alien landing strips. I know the pattern. I don't have to be airborne to recognize it. It's Heruka.

"I have been doing the practice of One with the Heruka gong to shatter all illusions..." I recall Evan's words to me.

I first encountered the myths of Heruka when I was a boy. My dad had a pretty intense library. On days with nothing to do I would take down a book and just start reading wherever it opened. I didn't always like to read from the first to last page. Sometimes I enjoyed just tasting parts of a book. It was on one of those lazy days when a book on spirituality opened to a chapter on a Wakkism deity called Heruka. "Heruka: The Blood Drinker."

I didn't believe in any of those legends, but the Heruka chap-

ters amazed me. I was drawn to Heruka because his legend was

like poetry, a beautiful union of opposites. I remember a quote

from the book, "Where opposites meet truth lays."

Heruka represents the merging of life and death, and thus they

cancel each other out, which leaves a perpetual bliss state. He is

beyond Earth and Heaven. He is a deity that is capable of re-

moving all illusion. Heruka can unfasten any false notion of life,

death, and Heaven.

Heruka is a blood drinking god, but he does this for the bene-

fit of all beings, by draining the illusion, not unlike a witch-

doctor sucking the poison from a snake bite.

It is taught that the syllables of his name represents the truth.

"HE-," represents the emptiness of life phenomenon. "RU-,"

represents the emptiness of being, as life is the greatest illusion

of all, it is nothing more than a breeze blowing through a ghost

town. "KA," represents true, absolute, bliss.

Illusion is his enemy. The goal is to stamp out the illusion of

birth and death, breaking a cycle, in order to create a true perpetual bliss state. This is why Heruka is one of the most worshiped

gods in Wakkism.

I was too young to understand the complex rites and mean-

ings that encompassed the legends of Heruka. Later, I was pre-

occupied with my own life and suffering. I forgot about the

teachings in that book all together. I could do with them now.

The Seagull

I enter the clearing and walk among the stones. I do not understand any of the symbols that cover them. I make my way to the middle point of the clearing and find the center stone. I crouch down to get a better look. I do recognize one symbol on this stone. There is a figure of a seagull carved near the top of the stone.

In my mind I return to the day after graduation when Drew and I were on the beach. I was writing poetry and Drew was watching the birds that hovered above us. The sky was so blue and the sun warmed the sand. The breeze from the ocean kept us cool. Drew turned his attention away from the sky and asked me to write a poem about the seagulls.

"It doesn't work that way." I said

"Why not?"

"Because, I have to be moved, be inspired... then the words come. Why seagulls anyway?"

He turned his attention back to the sky, watching the birds and said, *"They are so free, just flying all day without effort; they barely even have to beat their wings. And, their songs move me; their calls are so empty, no sadness or happiness, nothing good or bad, so beautifully empty. Don't ya think?"*

I plopped my pad and pen down, rolled over onto my back and gazed upon the birds. Drew moved closer to me and rested his hand on my belly, this filled my entire body with a warmth. I put my arm around his neck and pulled him against me. We laid listening to the songs of the seagulls.

While crouching in front of the seagull symbol a soft blue light illuminates the stone, as the light grows brighter I realize it's my necklace. The brilliance clears my head. Realization comes galloping to the front of my mind.

Of course, it all makes sense. Drew's love of seagulls. His present to me that I hung above my death bath, it was the last image I saw as I died. Now, it's my glowing charm. The seagulls at the Thrift Shop. He's trying to show me the way to him, but I'm to wrapped up in my own shit to have seen the signs.

My way to Drew has been around my neck, so close I missed it. This is why Book wanted the necklace. He never had any intension of bringing me to Drew, just the opposite, he tried to drive me away.

The Battle

Anger grows inside; it's tearing me apart, but I let it come. My head feels like it is going to split open. I grab my head falling to my knees. *Shit, it is splitting open.*

The forest and stones tilt as the space between my eyes grows. I'm seeing the world like a googly-eyed reptile. Teeth separate, followed by my lips, while my tongue splits down the middle. My neck opens, but is tethered by my chain.

Blood spills, soaking the forest floor. Ribs pop and snap. I feel a heavy weight cutting through me. No, out of me. *Oh God, it's like giving fucking birth.* I fall to the ground, exhausted, as my body seals shut. Feet stand before me. I smell smoke. Book.

"Get u..."

Before he can finish his sentence I am up, standing behind him, with my claw at his throat.

"Don't you see? Or perhaps you do not?" He asks.

"I see. I see how fucked up you are."

"We are."

"We? No, not We. You."

"I can climb right out of your soul and you still do not fully comprehend who I am. I am you Bardo Boy. I am your essence. I am what makes you, you. Without me you are nothing. I was the one who filled your life and death with purpose and meaning. There is no you without me."

Bereft of any hesitation, my claw opens his throat. I let Book fall to the ground as I turn and walk away. I start my new journey without Book, while I walk I feel a searing pain below my chin, stumbling, I catch myself against one of the stones. I grab my neck, it's moist with blood. I look back at Book. He is rising. His wound, as mine, is already healing. Book is up and

facing me.

"Kill me and you kill yourself," he says, shaken.

I have never seen Book this unnerved, but I know he's a liar.

I charge him again, moving like a flash of light. He stands there,

while my claw enters his chest, there's no bone, no blood, no

heart. Nevertheless, Book is experiencing some distress, weak-

ening. Searing pain again. A hole opens in my chest as I spill

blood. Staggering, I remove my fist from Book and the wounds

close.

We fall to the ground. Drained, I press myself up onto my

hands and knees, crawling towards Book. He's not putting up a

fight. He just keeps taking it, or is it me who takes the beating?

On top of him, I look down. His hair has come undone, his

finely pressed clothes are tattered. I bring my clenched claw-fist

up towards the trees, then drive it down into Book's face. I am

the one who takes the blow. But, I don't care. *It's all a trick...* I can beat my way through this illusion, but with every strike to

Book's face I am equally damaged. I keep going, until my face

is so bloodied that I can't see my target. It's now me who is on

the ground. The forest spins, while darkness comes and goes.

Book rises.

"*Isn't this enough Bardo Boy?*" Book asks, as he fixes his tie

and smoothes back his hair, "*Now it is my turn.*" The ground

rumbles and heaves, knocking over stones with each swell. "*We*

are indivisible. That is just how it is, this is the nature of our

relationship, it is the nature of our existence..."

Tree roots break up through the forest's floor and entwine my

legs, arms, and neck. My chest heaves and opens wide, as I

howl in pain. Book lies on top of me, groin to groin. He takes

hold of by biceps and brings his lips to mine, as if giving me a

final kiss. He enters me through the wound in my chest. My

chest seals shut as my hair changes from black to blonde. My

clothes simmer away, a suit replaces them. I am becoming

Book. Tears come to my eyes as I think about Drew. I'll never see him again.

INTER-BARDO LOG #3

"OM SHRI VAJRA HE HE RU RU KA KA. OM SHRI VAJRA HE HE RU RU KA KA. OM SHRI VAJRA HE HE RU RU KA KA. OM SHRI VAJRA HE HE RU RU KA KA. OM SHRI VAJRA HE HE RU RU KA KA. OM SHRI VAJRA HE HE RU RU KA KA. OM SHRI VAJRA HE HE RU RU KA KA. OM SHRI VAJRA HE HE RU RU KA KA. OM SHRI VAJRA HERUKA!

Together we have completed the Heruka mantra. Your reading of the words and my prayers have brought us closer. Heruka is destroying all the illusions that separate us, merging our worlds. I am in your mind and you are in my mind. Through you, I know all that has happened to Bardo Boy. It is more difficult for you to know my mind. I am Evan, a family friend of Bardo Boy. I see, you know this already. We are closer than I thought.

I understand that you believe that this story is fictional. On one hand this is true, but as you read you create a new world in your mind; a world that makes memories. Who is to say which memory is more real, a memory from your life or a memory from a story? Memories are mischievous spirits, even when false they can have tangible consequences.

END INTER-BARDO LOG #3

Home

Book rises fully restored and produces a cigarette. He lights it and takes a deep drag as the end glows a bright red. A smokey cloud billows from his lips as the glowing from the cigarette gets brighter and brighter. But, it's not a red luminosity, it's blue. Book drops his cigarette and looks down towards his chest. The blue brilliance is coming from under his shirt. He rips it open to find the seagull necklace hanging from his neck.

"Fucking necklace," Book says, as he struggles to tear it from his neck. The more he strives, like a cat when given its first taste of a collar, the brighter it glows. It's now Book who is experiencing pain. He lets out a roar as blue light splits open his chest. I jump out of my cell, the body of Book, and roll out onto the ground. I take for the forest like a rabbit being hunted by a pack of dogs. I am trying to make as much distance between Book and me. The air grows frigid as I run.

I travel over empty logs that lay rotten on the forest floor.

Grounded, motionless, strapped down with a seasonless growth

of ivy that seems never to die, never seems alive either. Fungi

with dry rot mustiness, various hues of blue, and green, and

white, coating the insides, crumbly, clingy.

I don't know where I'm heading, but the thoughtless motion is

comforting. While running, I feel a sharp whip like sensation

against my cheek. Followed by stillness, then strangulation. I'm

airborne. A large tendril from a tree has me about the neck. The

forest disappears as I lose consciousness.

"Smiley, come on you'll be late for school." I feel my toes

being shaken. When I open my eyes I see a pillow and sheets

about me. Startled, I sit up and feel the bed with my hands and

touch my neck. *"Are you ok? You must have been having quite*

the dream. Come on, get up. Breakfast is ready. You better get

up before Paul eats all the toast."

"Paul?"

My mom is standing at the foot of my bed. *"Come on,"* she says as she exits my room. Before leaving she turns and says, *"Oh, Drew called for you this morning, I told him you where sleeping. He said for me to tell you to call him."*

"Drew?"

She turns back towards me, *"You certainly are odd this morning. Hurry, you don't want to miss your graduation."*

"Graduation...not that again." My mom shakes her head in annoyance as she turns, *"Get up, now!"* Scolding me as she leaves.

I can't believe I am lying in my bed, in my old bedroom. *Was it all a dream?* I throw the cover back and head to the cork board on the wall across the room. It's filled with my poems, some done formally on neat white paper, others written hurriedly on scraps, only partially finished. I enjoy reading them again. It

has been such a long time since I saw them.

I pull one of the poems off the board. It's titled *Wake up!*

Wake up! I don't remember writing this one. If I didn't know

better, I'd think is was my mom's work, written this morning and

hung for me to see.

Wake up! Wake up!

You are not who you think you are, your friends

are not who they think they are...

You are being held prisoner in a cage without bars.

This is the only way to get my message

to you!

Wake up! Wake up!

My mom has put out my graduation suit. The cap and gown hang on the back of the door. I wash up, get dressed, and head downstairs. The smell of the eggs and toast brings on instant hunger. Paul is sitting at the kitchen table with Derry. Derry, as always, is by Paul's chair waiting for a hand to come down with a piece of toast. I walk over to my mother and put my arms around her. I bury my face into her, loving her scent.

"I love you Mom."

She puts her hands around me and squeezes me tight. Paul's turn, I give him a big choke-hold hug and kiss him on the top of his head, messing his hair. He pushes me away, annoyed, but I can tell he loves the attention. I steal a piece of toast from his plate, take a bite and throw it to Derry.

"Hey, I was going to eat that." Paul blurts out.

"Like it wasn't going to end up in Derry's belly anyway."

"You look so handsome in your suit. I'm so proud of you,"

mom says to me.

My dream is fading away as practical matters take hold of my

mind. I have to remember to bring my cap and gown, call

Drew... In mid-thought I ask, *"Where's Dad? Is he taking us to*

school today for graduation?"

"Oh, Smiley. I'm so sorry. I thought I told you last week that

Dad wouldn't be here for your graduation. He left early this

morning. We're going to take the bus today." She says, as she

kisses my forehead.

"But, he said I could borrow the car this week." I say with

disappointment.

"Go into the dining room, he left a present for you."

Dragging my feet I go into the dining room. There is large book on the table. Although it's wrapped, I know it's a book by its shape. I undo the paper, curious to see what book my dad has picked out for me. The book looks antique. Leather bound. "The Book of Bardo" is stamped into the leather cover. I start to open it, but mom reminds us of the time. I close the book and set it back down on the table.

"I have to call Drew." I say, remembering my mom's message.

"We don't have time now, you'll see him at graduation. I need you to help Paul get ready for school, his bus should be here any minute."

Morning rush hour is upon us. Derry is let outside to do his business. Paul struggles with his heavy backpack. It is his last day of school and all the books must be returned.

We head to the bus stop. It is several windy blocks away, about a twenty minute walk. It's unseasonably cool for a summer day, frigid. I welcome the cool day since I am wearing a suit. While walking the wind tries to take my plastic covered gown. It flaps behind me like a kite on a short tether.

The road is tree lined. The towering trees look ancient, they stand like a row of guards on each side of the street, swaying in the cool breeze. We arrive at the bus stop. We are accompanied by two older women that were here before us. The two look misplaced from time. Pillbox hats, black patent leather purses dangle from their forearms, and old lady shoes with thick heels. The two women take turns stepping to the curb and looking down the street for the bus, then at their watches.

"The bus is never on time." One says to the other.

They continue this ritual every thirty seconds or so. I look at my watch. The bus isn't late at all, still has a minute or so. I think about their experience of reality, living in a world where the bus is always late when it is not. A world created by them that is real enough to cause discomfort, but is not based on any truth. *There's a poem here somewhere.*

While I wait for the poem to arrive and the bus, I notice the advertisement on the wall at the end of the bus portico. It's a large movie poster. "Wake up! Wake up! Coming this summer!" There is a photo of a man with fangs; he is clad in leather boots, pants, and jacket. His clothes are adorned with skull and bones. I think about the poem on my bedroom wall. I'm trying to connect the poster and poem, as the bus pulls up.

I'm dazed. I know the bus is here, but I am stuck in my thoughts. My mom jostles me to get on the bus. The two old ladies are already aboard. We take a seat on a bench that runs lengthwise. Street scenes become less rural and more city as the bus moves. Shops line the street, nail salon, convenience market, flooring and tile store, liquor store...

"Is that Patty Shoemaker?" My mom asks. *"I think she trying to get that man to buy her alcohol! I want you to stay away from her Smiley."*

No need to tell me that. Her body odor alone is enough to keep me away. Being her tenth grade locker partner was enough Patty Shoemaker for a life time. My mind leaves Patty at the liquor store and returns to the "Wake Up" movie poster and my poem. Strange, *I don't remember writing the poem.* Why would I write about a movie that isn't out yet.

I get up from my seat leaving the gown in place, I make my way to the two old women. Standing in front of them, they return my stare with their own curious gazes.

"Wake up! Wake up!" I say to them, then, *"You are not who you think you are, and the bus wasn't late!"* Their eyes retreat under their forehead leaving skin covered craters where sockets and eyeballs once where, their mouths widen to expose rows and rows of teeth. They are attached at the sides like siamese twins. In unison they say to me, *"Your the one who needs to wake up... Boy!"*

I'm startled by my mom's elbow tapping at my side, as I am still seated next to her. She's letting me know that we've arrived.

I must have been daydreaming. I look down the aisle, the two old ladies are exiting the bus. We catch up.

I hop off the last step, when one of the two women turns to me and says, "*I have a granddaughter graduating today. It should be a wonderful day beings its not too hot. Good luck with your graduation...Boy.*" They chuckle and walk away.

I could have sworn I saw several rows of teeth. *Did she call me Boy?* Naw, It must have been her loose dentures giving her a toothy look, old people sometimes do call younger guys, "boy."

Graduation

The bus stop is right in front of the high school. Seniors are everywhere, some heading into the building with parents, others standing on the side of the school in groups with their year books, exchanging signatures. I definitely do not belong in any of the groups. Everyone is feeling the chill this morning, huddled a little closer than personal distance would normally allow. I look out over all the kids, I am trying to spot Drew in the crowds.

I turn to my mom and ask, *"Did Drew say where he'd meet us?"*

"No, he wanted you to call him is all." She replies.

I knew I should have taken the time to call him. I'm never going to find him in this herd. I'm aggravated with my mother and myself for not calling Drew. While I scan the landscape I feel a hand touch my shoulder. I turn, it's Drew. We grasp each other in a firm hug.

"You two act like you haven't seen each other for years. Really you both need to get girlfriends." My mom says to us.

"Mom I have something to tell you." I say to her as Drew looks at me.

"What is it Smiley?"

"You better sit down for this." I say as her stare grows more serious. *"I asked Patty Shoemaker to marry me."*

"Oh, you." She says with a shove and smile. *"You two better get inside. I'll meet you back here after the ceremony. I love you. You make me so proud, Smiley."*

Walking into the school Drew asks me, *"What was that all about?"* I tell him about my mom seeing Patty trying to buy alcohol at the liquor store on the way here. *"Really?"* He says to me with a shit-eating grin on his face, as we're walking into the school I spot Patty.

"Speaking of the devil." I say to Drew. He looks up and sees Patty entering the building.

"I'll meet you inside." Drew says to me, with his grin growing more devilish.

Before I can ask him to wait he is off and running. I drift though the front doors on my own like a ghost. The hallway wall holds the seating charts for the ceremony. I find my place on the map, then look for Drew's. I'm hoping we'll be next to each other. *"Fuck."* We couldn't be further apart. Alone again. The hallway is crowded, but I might as well be the only one here, as no one even notices me. I reposition my cap and gown and squeeze down the hall through the maze of students, making my way to the auditorium.

The auditorium is also the gymnasium. There is a stage on one side used for the school plays, battle of the bands, and talent shows. The ends have retractable basketball hoops, which are in the up position today. The walls opposite the stage have roll out bleachers that fold up into large wooden cabinets during gym.

The bleachers are filling up with parents, siblings, aunts, uncles, and grandparents. Metal chairs fill the gymnasium floor, each has a number that corresponds to the wall charts in the hallway.

I find my seat at the end of the row, release my cap and gown from its plastic tomb, put it on over my suit and sit down. I scan the gym looking for Drew, but there is no sign of him. The seats begin to fill up, making it harder for me to find him. I have an idea where he is sitting, from looking at the wall charts, but there are so many seats. A loud buzz, crack, and stuttering fills the air, it is followed by, *"Can everyone please take a seat so we can get started."*

Graduation begins with principle Bartrum calling all to order. His voice drones on becoming a blah, blah, blah, garble, garble, garble, while I check-out the stage. It's decorated with balloons, paper streamers, signs of congratulations, and a forest setting.

Forest setting?

The back of the stage has the remains of the last play. Funny, that they haven't taken it down for graduation. Large brown paper trunks topped with green paper leaves and vines.

The larger trees are up front, on the outer edges. The trees get smaller as they move to the black center, creating a vantage point. It gives the illusion of depth.

Principle Bartrum's voice is replaced with clicking, creeping, whooping, hissing, and rattling, as I look into the black center. The longer I stare at the forest scene, the more alive it becomes. There is something hanging from a vine in the black center.

I jump when I feel a arm come around my neck. It's Drew, with his diploma in hand.

"What are you doing man? Wake up, go and get it. Meet me under the bleachers by the locker room when you're done, I have a surprise for you."

My row is already heading for the stage to get their diplomas. I catch up to them. While climbing the stage I take a better look at the forest. Up close it looks like a cheap high school set. I'm next to get my diploma. Principle Bartrum turns with my diploma in hand, he has a big toothy smile, his eyes are fleshed over.

"Congratulations...Boy," he says to me. I break out in a sweat, grab the scroll, and blast off the stage onto the gymnasium floor. My heart is beating through my chest. *What did Mom put on that toast?*

I spot the locker room and head to the bleachers to meet Drew. I want to tell Drew what just happened, but seeing him there, squatting against the wall looking so good, pacifies me.

When I'm with Drew the world is right. He sees me coming and stands up with a huge smile. I navigate the metal straps of the bleacher supports to meet him by the wall. Standing in front of him, looking into his eyes, banishes my anxiety. He grabs me by the front of my gown and leads me away. His touch sends a horny wave through my body.

"Follow me." He says with a alluring smile. That smile always sucks me in. My gown still in his grasp, he pulls me into the men's locker room around the corner. In the locker room, he spins me around and presses his body against mine until I am pinned against the cold tile wall.

He reaches under his gown and produces a bottle of blackberry brandy. He takes a mouth full and passes me the bottle. I don't care about drinking that much, Drew is my drink and whatever makes him happy makes me happy. The blackberry brandy is overly sweat, as if the syrup was there to cover the taste of the cheap alcohol used to make it, which it doesn't, it tastes like cough syrup. But, I drink because Drew drinks.

"What do you want to do tomorrow now that we're free?" He asks, after taking another large swig.

"I don't know, I'm not really thinking about tomorrow."

"Let's go down the shore"

"Sounds good to me. Wait, my dad left town with the car. We have no way of getting down there."

"Well, let's just hang out at your house." His second offer.

He looks into my eyes as he presses himself against me and brings his lips to mine. The bottle of brandy presses painfully into my back. But, I don't care, because it feels so good when he holds me tight.

He takes my upper lip between his teeth and grabs me tighter. He holds me in his arms and mouth as if we would never see each other again. Our embrace brakes when the door to the locker room flies open. It's Patty, my old locker mate. When she sees us against the wall she halts in her hunt and screams,

"Queers." She runs out onto the gym floor to blast the news of what she had just seen.

Drew grabs me by my hand and we make our exit. We run down the hall that leads from the gym to the outside courts behind the school, we tear around the side of the school to the front. The ceremony is letting out. Winded, we join my mom where we had left her. She gives us a big hug.

"What's that I smell? Have you boys been drinking?" She asks sternly.

"Ah, nope." I say fumbling. My mom gives me a suspicious look.

Drew kicks in, *"It was Patty Shoemaker. To be honest Mrs H., we where teasing her. She got mad and pulled out a bottle of booze from under her gown and threw it at us. It smashed on the wall, booze went everywhere."*

"I knew she was buying liquor this morning. My future daughter-in-law. You better have been kidding Smiley."

"Can Drew come over for dinner and spend the night?" I ask, quickly changing the subject.

"If it's ok with Drew's mom." She replies.

"No problem Mrs. H., my folks are ok with it." Drew says, lying through his teeth. He hasn't even spoken with them. Both of Drew's parents have a drinking problem. That gives Drew a long leash. He doesn't really like living at home. He spends a lot of time by us.

"Are your parents here Drew? I haven't seen them."

"Naw. They both couldn't get out of work today." Drew says, continuing the lies.

The Book

The bus pulls up and we all board. After a bumpy bus ride and stroll down the tree lined street, we're home. We walk through the door, Derry jumps on Drew. I'm thinking, I can't wait until I can jump him.

"Get down Derry." My mom says as she drags Derry outside. In Derry's excitement he dribbles a little pee, *"Smiley, can you wipe that up please."* She says, as she exits the door. I clean up the pee while Drew heads into the dining room.

"What's this?" He asks.

I turn to see him holding my book. *"It's my graduation present from my Dad,"* I answer, joining him in the dining room.

"It looks old." He says to me.

I grab the book and motion to Drew to follow me upstairs to my room. In my room, I close the door and we jump into bed. Drew, me, and the book. Lying together I open the book. Drew quickly closes it, moves it to the side and lies on top of me. He buries his groin into mine while his hand reaches up under my shirt.

Just as he is about to kiss me we hear a rumbling flying up the steps. Drew rolls off me onto the floor. I pull down my shirt and flip open the book as the door flies open. It's Paul, home from his last day at school. He is looking pretty happy. He spots Drew on the floor.

"Hi Drew," Paul blurts out.

"Hey Paul, what's up?"

"What are you guys doin?" Paul asks

"Reading." I say

"Why is Drew on the floor?" Another Paul question.

"Because, he likes it there. Don't you believe in knocking

first?" I say, as I get up and usher Paul out of the room. Drew

and I look at each other and laugh. I return to the bed. The book

is open to a figure of a four headed god. I pick up the book. The

title above the figure reads, "HERUKA."

I look down at Drew. The expression on his face has

changed. He looks sad. Before I can process his change in emo-

tion the room grows dark. Drew covers his face and cowers

against the dresser. I can barely make him out as the room dark-

ens.

The bed, my room, and the house break away from me. Sus-

pended by my neck, I am back in the forest. I still have the book

in one of my hands, while my other hand clutches at the vine that

is snaring my throat.

I squeeze the vine, crushing it. It releases its hold dropping

me to the forest floor. I land on my feet holding the book. The

ground is snow covered and the air is cold. I can see my breath as it leaves my lungs. My fury swells like a tormented bull in a ring. Steam bellows from my nostril and mouth. It was all an illusion, another diversion by Book. I was never home.

Yet, something broke his hold on me. Something is keeping Book from totally taking me over. Book isn't invincible. We must be equals. I run over the events leading to the clearing. It's when I saw the stones laid out into the symbol of Heruka. I was regretting I didn't pay more attention to the book in my dad's library, but here it is now. Somehow, I have pulled it out of thin air.

The memories of just being with Drew, my Mom, and Paul are playing in my head. The time line was altered from the original memory I had of those days, a dream within a dream? Was it changed for Book's needs or a tug of war of some sort? It seemed so real, but it wasn't. Yet, I have the Book of Bardo in my hand, proof that it did happen.

Bliss vs. Love

The air is biting. The wind surges, while snow fills the sky. The trees are frozen, some remain standing while others drop. I hear a loud crack, like lightning splitting wood, when one large tree falls next to me. It shatters into a thousand puzzle pieces. I have to get out of the forest, before I'm crushed.

Holding the Book of Bardo tight against my side, racing to the edge of the forest, I dodge trees as they tumble and fall. As I reach the tree line, I'm slammed by an invisible wall and thrown back into the forest. My head is spinning. Through the vertigo I see Book standing in front of me. The Book of Bardo is on the ground between us.

"Not so fast Bardo Boy, let's talk this over, just you and I."

I've lost. Evan was right, Book is my prison keeper.

The wind gusts, it blows open the Book of Bardo. We look at the opening pages as they come to rest. Before us is the page that ended my dream with Drew, in my bedroom. The four headed god, Heruka, is clearly visible.

Evan's words return to me, *"The bardos are the hardest prisons to escape, because you do not even know you are being held."* I look onto the page.

"Stop it Boy. Stop it right now." Book demands. He makes a rush for the Book of Bardo and seizes it.

Illusions evaporate like a morning mist burned away by the rising sun. Looking into the trees, I know they are me. *It's all me.* I raise my arm as a large icy tendril uncoils, it dives down through the frozen leaves and snares Book around his arm. I summon another, it grabs Book by his other arm, making him drop the Book of Bardo.

Snow crystals, covering the ground, sparkle as I walk towards Book. His appearance is in shambles. He tries to kick me as I approach him. The ground rumbles as I bring up roots to secure his legs. The Book of Bardo lays next to his foot. Book breathes heavy as he struggles.

"I guess you would be wanting one of your cigarettes about now?"

"Bardo Boy, listen to me. You want Drew, because he brings you happiness. It is happiness you seek; I can make you happy."

"Fuck you."

I turn and leave with the Book of Bardo, opening it to the chapter on Heruka, when a loud snap rings out and a penetrating pain enters my back, the Book of Bardo flies from my hands. Looking down I have a large icy tendril exiting my chest. *"It's all me, just my mind. There is no icy tendril."* With that thought my injury fades. I turn and find Book has freed himself, he holds

a broken piece of tendril.

"You don't give up," I say to Book

"Never." He screams at me.

The Book of Bardo lay on the ground open to the page I

sought. "HERUKA." We both stare down at it as Book backs

away.

I start to speak his name. With the leaving of the first syllable

from my lips a reverberation is produced, the wind takes the

sound and distributes it thought the forest.

"He... He he he he... He he he he... He he he he..."

When the waves of sound reach Book he's transformed into

solid ice. The echo of Heruka's first syllable passes Book, enter-

ing the icy trees as they burst into frozen powder. The uttering of just part of his name exposes the illusion of phenomenon and obliterates it.

Evan sits on a tile floor, in a bathroom that is forming around him. His legs are crossed with his palms resting on his knees. His lips move with a rhythm as he chants.

I speak the second syllable, *"Ru."* Ru rolls off my tongue as the purest of truths ever spoken. *"Ru ru ru... Ru ru ru ru...,"* follows the previous syllable. Again, the vibrations are carried by the wind, they expose the empty nature of all things. The sound reaches Book, he explodes into a icy dust cloud. The ice cloud sublimates and he is gone. The emptiness spreads clearing away the forest, ground, and sky.

Walls become solid as Evan continues his prayers.

The last syllable, *"Ka, ka, ka...,"* is spoken as euphoria blooms within me. An insurmountable joy replaces all that was once there.

Prior, there had been moments of joy, pain, or suffering. Each cycling around and through me. When joy came I couldn't imagine it leaving, but it did. The same with pain. Endless cycles of joy and pain are now replaced with emptiness. It's a hollowing that leaves a space to be filled with joy. The joy of nothing. True bliss. True freedom.

In my bathroom, back in my apartment. I am sitting naked on the edge of the tub, my death bath. One wall of the bathroom is replaced with a blissful light. The wall's surface radiates an undulating shimmer that awakens joy with each ripple. Every moment of my life and death merge. *It all leads to here.* The brilliance overtakes me and I remember. *I am the light.*

Evan is here, seated on the floor. *"My prayers have made their way to you. This has helped awaken the dreamer. You are no longer the dream or the dreamer. You have found your prison walls and broke through them. You have completed your cycles.*

I am overjoyed for you."

Standing up from the side of the tub, to merge with the Bliss
State, I spot the seagull rope soap dangling from the faucet and
pause.

"Drew hasn't passed his test, has he?" I ask Evan

*"Probably not, but that doesn't mean he will not, someday.
I'm sure he was born again."*

*"I can't do it, not without Drew. He has been with me through
everything, my life, my death, my illusions. I can't abandon
him."* While I tell Evan this, the water in the bath glows a dim
blue.

*"I have no say in this, but remember there has only been a few
out of unknowable numbers that have been offered the Bliss State*

by Heruka. To throw it away, and for what? Love, or what you

think love is? It is your decision. I pass no judgment. The Book

of Bardo tells us the unfolding of the Universe is perfection in-

carnate, it is our view of the unfolding that is flawed. It is your

choice."

The bright light fades into a solid wall, while I fall backwards

into my glowing blue death bath.

A bloated naked body is submerged in a bathtub. Face up, its

eyes are blackened with death. The skin is soft and loose, about

to come away from the bone. Shit expelled at the time of death is

now completely dissolved giving the water a stagnant, pond

scum, quality. Fumes rise from the water and fill the tiny bath-

room with an odor that could cause instant spewing; it smells

like shit mixed with burnt hair. Flies teem on the window and

bathtub, lapping up the encrusted scum that is caked on the

sides. Shit water whirlpools, cleansing itself of pollutants as it

swirls...

Darkness, aqueous, bobbing, squeezing, uterus, ...*all the blood*, bright light, rubber fingers, breath, hunger, then sleep.

Consciousness comes for only short moments, mostly when I am hungry, cold, or in pain. I'm unable to control my head, arms, or legs. Occasionally, I catch a glimpse of birds over me, then sleep overcomes me again.

A young woman who is only days home from the hospital enters the room to bask in the joy her new son brings her. She has adorned the room with decorations of the beach. Blue ocean waves are painted on the walls, along with sand pails and shovels. She has placed a mobile over her son's crib, from it dangles plastic Seagulls.

"The end is just another beginning..."-The Book of Bardo

Made in the USA